MR. VERDANT GREEN,
MARRIED AND DONE FOR

Oxford student Verdant Green and his sisters travel to spend their summer at Honeywood Hall in Northumbria, where our hero is captivated by the young daughter of the house, the vivacious and charming Miss Patty: accomplished horse-woman, sketcher and water-colourist. A warm regard springs up between the two, and Verdant dares to hope that something more than friendship may result. But when Patty's cousin, the handsome and confident Frank Delaval, arrives to stay, Verdant suspects he has a rival for Miss Patty's affections. Will he gracefully concede defeat — or end up married and done for?

CUTHBERT BEDE

MR. VERDANT GREEN, MARRIED AND DONE FOR

Complete and Unabridged

ULVERSCROFT
Leicester

First published in Great Britain in 1857

This Large Print Edition
published 2016

A catalogue record for this book is available
from the British Library.

3\16

ISBN 978–1–4448–2756–9

Published by
F. A. Thorpe (Publishing)
Anstey, Leicestershire

Set by Words & Graphics Ltd.
Anstey, Leicestershire
Printed and bound in Great Britain by
T. J. International Ltd., Padstow, Cornwall

This book is printed on acid-free paper

Chapter

1

Mr. Verdant Green Travels North

July: fierce and burning!

A day to tinge the green corn with a golden hue. A day to scorch grass into hay between sunrise and sunset. A day in which to rejoice in the cool thick masses of trees, and to lie on one's back under their canopy, and look dreamily up, through its rents, at the peep of hot, cloudless, blue sky. A day to sit on shady banks upon yielding cushions of moss and heather, from whence you gaze on bright flowers blazing in the blazing sun, and rest your eyes again upon your book to find the lines swimming in a radiance of mingled green and red. A day that fills you with amphibious feelings, and makes you desire to be even a dog, that you might bathe and paddle and swim in every roadside brook and pond, without the exertion of dressing and undressing, and yet with propriety. A day that sends you out by willow-hung streams, to fish, as an excuse for idleness. A day that drives you dinnerless from smoking joints, and plunges you thirstfully into barrels of beer. A day that induces apathetic listlessness and total prostration of energy, even under the aggravating warfare of gnats and wasps. A day that engenders pity for the ranks of ruddy haymakers, hotly marching on under the merciless glare of the noonday sun. A day when the very air, steaming up from the earth, seems to palpitate with the heat. A day when Society has left its cool and pleasant country-house, and finds itself baked and burnt up in town, condemned to ovens of operas, and fiery furnaces of *levees* and drawing-rooms. A day when even ice is warm, and perspiring visitors to the Zoological Gardens envy the hippopotamus living in his bath. A day when a hot, frizzling, sweltering smell ascends from the ground, as though it was the earth's great ironing day. And — above all — a day that converts a railway traveller into a martyr, and a first-class carriage into a moving representation of the Black Hole of Calcutta.

So thought Mr. Verdant Green, as he was whirled onward to the far north, in company with his three sisters, Miss Bouncer, and Mr. Charles Larkyns. Being six in number, they formed a snug (and hot) family party, and filled the carriage, to the exclusion of little Mr. Bouncer, who, nevertheless, bore this temporary and unavoidable separation with a tranquil mind, inasmuch as it enabled him to ride in a second-class carriage, where he could the more conveniently indulge in the furtive pleasures of the Virginian weed. But, to keep up his connection with the party, and to prove that his interest in them could not be diminished by a brief and enforced absence, Mr. Bouncer paid them flying visits at every station, keeping his pipe alight by a puff into the carriage, accompanied with an expression of his full conviction that Miss Fanny Green had been smoking, in defiance of the company's by-laws. These rapid interviews were enlivened by Mr. Bouncer informing his friends that Huz and Buz (who were panting in a locker) were as well as could be expected, and giving any other interesting particulars regarding himself, his fellow-travellers, or the country in general, that could be compressed into the space of sixty seconds or thereabouts; and the visits were regularly and ruthlessly brought to an abrupt termination by the angry 'Now, then, sir!' of the guard, and the reckless thrusting of the little gentleman into his second-class carriage, to the endangerment of his life and limbs, and the exaggerated display of authority on the part of the railway official.

Mr. Bouncer's mercurial temperament had enabled him to get over the little misfortune that had followed upon his examination for his degree; but he still preserved a memento of that hapless period in the shape of a wig of curly black hair. For he found, during the summer months, such coolness from his shaven poll, that, in spite of 'the mum's' entreaties, he would not suffer his own luxuriant locks to grow, but declared that, till the winter at any rate, he would wear his gent's real head of hair; and in order that our railway party should not forget the reason for its existence, Mr. Bouncer occasionally favoured them with a sight of his bald head, and also narrated to them, with great glee, how, when a very starchy lady of a certain age had left their carriage, he had called after her upon the platform — holding out his wig as he did so — that she had left some of her property behind her; and how the passengers and porters had grinned, and the starchy lady had lost all her stiffening through the hotness of her wrath.

York at last! A half-hour's escape from the hot carriage, and a hasty dinner on cold lamb and cool salad in the pleasant refreshment-room hung round with engravings. Mr. Bouncer's dinner is got over with incredible rapidity, in order that the little gentleman may carry out his humane intention of releasing Huz and Buz from their locker, and giving them their dinner and a run on the remote end of the platform, at a distance from timid spectators; which design is satisfactorily performed, and crowned with a douche bath from the engine-pump.

Then, away again to the rabbit-hole of a locker, the smoky second-class carriage, and the stuffy first-class; incarcerated in which black-hole, the plump Miss Bouncer, notwithstanding that she has removed her bonnet and all superfluous coverings, gets hotter than ever in the afternoon sun, and is seen, ever and anon, to pass over her glowing face a handkerchief cooled with the waters of Cologne. And, when the man with the grease-pot comes round to look at the tires of the wheels, the sight of it increases her warmth by suggesting a desire (which cannot be gratified) for lemon ice. Nevertheless, they have with them a variety of cooling refreshments, and their hothouse fruit and strawberries are most acceptable. The Misses Green have wisely followed their friend's example, in the removal of bonnets and mantles; and, as they amuse themselves with books and embroidery, the black-hole bears, as far as possible, a resemblance to a boudoir. Charles Larkyns favours the company with extracts from the *Times*; reads to them the last number of Dickens's new tale, or directs their attention to the most note-worthy points on their route. Mr. Verdant Green is seated *vis-a-vis* to the plump Miss Bouncer, and benignantly beams upon her through his glasses, or musingly consults his *Bradshaw* to count how much nearer they have crept to their destination, the while his thoughts have travelled on in the very quickest of express trains, and have already reached the far north.

Thus they journey: crawling under the stately old walls of York; then, with a rush and a roar, sliding rapidly over the level landscape, from whence they can look back upon the glorious Minster towers standing out grey and cold from the sunlit plain. Then, to Darlington; and on by porters proclaiming the names of stations in uncouth Dunelmian tongue, informing passengers that they have reached 'Faweyill' and 'Fensoosen,' instead of 'Ferry Hill' and 'Fence Houses,' and terrifying nervous people by the command to 'Change here for Doom!' when only the propinquity of the palatinate city is signified. And so, on by the triple towers of Durham that gleam in the sun with a ruddy orange hue; on, leaving to the left that last resting-place of Bede and St. Cuthbert, on the rock

'Where his cathedral, huge and vast,
Looks down upon the Wear.'

On, past the wonderfully out-of-place 'Durham monument,' a Grecian temple on a naked hill among the coal-pits; on, with a double curve, over the Wear, laden with its Rhine-like rafts; on, to grimy Gateshead and smoky Newcastle, and, with a scream and a rattle, over the wonderful High Level (then barely completed), looking down with a sort of self-satisfied shudder upon the bridge, and the Tyne, and the fleet of colliers, and the busy quays, and the quaint timber-built houses with their overlapping storys, and picturesque black and white gables. Then, on again, after a cool delay and brief release from the black-hole; on, into Northumbrian ground, over the Wansbeck; past Morpeth; by Warkworth, and its castle, and hermitage; over the Coquet stream, beloved by the friends of gentle Izaak Walton; on, by the sea-side — almost along the very sands — with the refreshing sea-breeze, and the murmuring plash of the breakers — the Misses Green giving way to childish delight at this their first glimpse of the sea; on, over the Aln, and past Alnwick; and so on, still further north, to a certain little station, which is the terminus of their railway journey, and the signal of their deliverance from the black-hole.

There, on the platform is Mr. Honeywood, looking hale and happy, and delighted to

7

receive his posse of visitors; and there, outside the little station, is the carriage and dog-cart, and a spring-cart for the luggage. Charles Larkyns takes possession of the dog-cart, in company with Mary and Fanny Green, and little Mr. Bouncer; while Huz and Buz, released from their weary imprisonment, caracole gracefully around the vehicle. Mr. Honeywood takes the reins of his own carriage; Mr. Verdant Green mounts the box beside him; Miss Bouncer and Miss Helen Green take possession of the open interior of the carriage; the spring-cart, with the servants and luggage, follows in the rear; and off they go.

But, though the two blood-horses are by no means slow of action, and do, in truth, gallop apace like fiery-footed steeds, yet to Mr. Verdant Green's anxious mind they seem to make but slow progress; and the magnificent country through which they pass offers but slight charms for his abstracted thoughts; until (at last) they come in sight of a broken mountain-range, and Mr. Honeywood, pointing with his whip, exclaims, 'Yon's the Cheevyuts, as they say in these parts; there are the Cheviot Hills; and there, just where you see that gleam of light on a white house among some trees — there is Honeywood Hall.'

Did Mr. Verdant Green remove his eyes from that object of attraction, save when intervening hills, for a time, hid it from his view? did he, when they neared it, and he saw its landscape beauties bathed in the golden splendours of a July sunset, did he think it a very paradise that held within its bowers the Peri of his heart's worship? did he — as they passed the lodge, and drove up an avenue of firs — did he scan the windows of the house, and immediately determine in his own mind which was HER window, oblivious to the fact that SHE might sleep on the other side of the building? did he, as they pulled up at the door, scrutinize the female figures who were there to receive them, and experience a feeling made up of doubt and certainty, that there was one who, though not present, was waiting near with a heart beating as anxiously as his own? did he make wild remarks, and return incoherent answers, until the long-expected moment had come that brought him face to face with the adorable Patty? did he envy Charles Larkyns for possessing and practising the cousinly privilege of bestowing a kiss upon her rosy cheeks? and did he, as he pressed her hand, and marked the heightened glow of her happy face, did he feel within his heart an exultant thrill of joy as the fervid thought fired his brain — one day she may be mine? Perhaps!

2

Mr. Verdant Green Delivers Miss Patty Honeywood from the Horns of a Dilemma

Even if Mr. Verdant Green had not been filled with the peculiarly pleasurable sensations to which allusion has just been made, it is yet exceedingly probable that he would have found his visit to Honeywood Hall one of those agreeable and notable events which the memory of after-years invests with the *couleur du rose*.

In the first place — even if Miss Patty was left out of the question — every one was so particularly attentive to him, that all his wants, as regarded amusement and occupation, were promptly supplied, and not a minute was allowed to hang heavily upon his hands. And, in the second place, the country, and its people and customs, had so much freshness and peculiarity, that he could not stir abroad without meeting with novelty. New ideas were constantly received; and other sensations of a still more delightful nature were daily deepened. Thus the time passed pleasantly away at Honeywood Hall, and the hours chased each other with flying feet.

Mr. Honeywood was a squire, or laird; and though the prospect from the hall was far too extensive to allow of his being monarch of *all* that he surveyed, yet he was the proprietor of no inconsiderable portion. The small village of Honeybourn, — which brought its one wide street of long, low, lime-washed houses hard by the hall, — owned no other master than Mr. Honeywood; and all its inhabitants were, in one way or other, his labourers. They had their own blacksmith, shoemaker, tailor, and carpenter; they maintained a general shop of the tea-coffee-tobacco-and-snuff genus; and they lived as one family, entirely independent of any other village. In fact, the villages in that district were as sparingly distributed as are 'livings' among poor curates, and, when met with, were equally as small; and so it happened, that as the landowners usually resided, like Mr. Honeywood, among their own people, a gentleman would occasionally be as badly off for a neighbour, as though he had been a resident in the backwoods of Canada. This evil, however, was productive of good, in that it set aside the possibility of a deliberate interchange of formal morning-calls, and obliged neighbours to be hospitable to each other, *sans ceremonie*, and with all good fellowship. To drive fifteen, twenty, or even five-and-twenty miles, to a dinner party was so common an occurrence, that it excited surprise only in a stranger, whose wonderment at this voluntary fatigue would be quickly dispelled on witnessing the hearty hospitality and friendly freedom that made a north country visit so enjoyable, and robbed the dinner party of its ordinary character of an English solemnity.

Close to Honeybourn village was the Squire's model farm, with its wide-spreading yards and buildings, and its comfortable bailiff's house. In a morning at sunrise, when our Warwickshire friends were yet in bed, such of them as were light sleepers would hear a not very melodious fanfare from a cow's horn — the signal to the village that the day's work was begun, which signal was repeated at sunset. This old custom possessed uncommon charms for Mr. Bouncer, whose only regret was that he had left behind him his celebrated tin horn. But he took to the cow-horn with the readiness of a child to a new plaything; and, having placed himself under the instruction of the Northumbrian Koenig, was speedily enabled to sound his octaves and go the complete unicorn (as he was wont to express it, in his peculiarly figurative eastern language) with a still more astounding effect than he had done on his former instrument. The little gentleman always made a point of thus signalling the times of the arrival and departure of the post, — greatly to the delight of small Jock Muir, who, girded with his letter-bag, and mounted on a highly-trained donkey, rode to and fro to the neighbouring post-town.

Although Mr. Verdant Green was not (according to Mr. Bouncer) 'a bucolical party,' and had not any very amazing taste for agriculture, he nevertheless could not but feel interested in what he saw around him. To one who was so accustomed to the small enclosures and timbered hedge-rows of the midland counties, the country of the Cheviots appeared in a grand, though naked aspect, like some stalwart gladiator of the stern old times. The fields were of large extent; and it was no uncommon sight to see, within one boundary fence, a hundred acres of wheat, rippling into mimic waves, like some inland sea. The flocks and herds, too, were on a grand scale; men counted their sheep, not by tens, but by hundreds. Everything seemed to be influenced, as it were, by the large character of the scenery. The green hills, with their short sweet grass, gave good pasture for the fleecy tribe, who were dotted over the sward in almost countless numbers; and Mr. Verdant Green was as much gratified with 'the silly sheep,' as with anything else that he witnessed in that land of novelty. To see the shepherd, with his bonnet and grey plaid, and long slinging step, walking first, and the flock following him, — to hear him call the sheep by name, and to perceive how he knew them individually, and how they each and all would answer to his voice, was a realization of Scripture reading, and a northern picture of Eastern life.

The head shepherd, old Andrew Graham — an active youth whose long snowy locks had been bleached by the snows of eighty winters — was an especial favourite of Mr. Verdant Green's, who would never tire of his company, or of his anecdotes of his marvellous dogs. His cottage was at a distance from the village, up in a snug hollow of one of the hills. There he lived, and there had been brought up his six sons, and as many daughters. Of the latter, two were out at service in noble families of the county; one was maid to the Misses Honeywood, and the three others were at home. How they and the other inmates of the cottage were housed, was a mystery; for, although old Andrew was of a superior condition in life to the other cottagers of Honeybourn, yet his domicile was like all the rest in its arrangements and accommodation. It was one moderately large room, fitted up with cupboards, in which, one above another, were berths, like to those on board a steamer. In what way the morning and evening toilettes were performed was a still greater mystery to our Warwickshire friends; nevertheless, the good-looking trio of damsels were always to be found neat, clean, and presentable; and, as their mother one day proudly remarked, they were 'douce, sonsy bairns, wi' weel-faur'd nebs; and, for puir folks, would be weel tochered.' Upon which our hero said 'Indeed!' which, as he had not the slightest idea what the good woman meant, was, perhaps, the wisest remark that he could have made.

One of them was generally to be found spinning at her muckle wheel, retiring and advancing to the music of its cheerful hum, the while her spun thread was rapidly coiled up on the spindle. The others, as they busied themselves in their household duties, or brightened up the delf and pewter, and set it out on the shelf to its best advantage, would join in some plaintive Scotch ballad, with such good taste and skill that our friends would frequently love to linger within hearing, though out of sight.

But these artless ditties were sometimes specially sung for them when they paid the cottage-room a visit, and sat around its canopied, projecting fire-place. For, old Andrew was a great smoker; and little Mr. Bouncer was exceedingly fond of waylaying him on his return home, and 'blowing a cloud' with so loquacious and novel a companion. And Mr. Verdant Green sometimes joined him in these visits; on which occasions, as harmony was the order of the day, he would do his best to further it by singing 'Marble Halls,' or any other song that his limited *repertoire* could boast; while old Andrew would burst into 'Tullochgorum,' or do violence to 'Get up and bar the door.'

It must be confessed, that the conversation at such times was sustained not without difficulty. Old Andrew, his wife, and the major portion of his family, were barely able to understand the language of their guests, whom they persisted in generalizing as 'cannie Soothrons;' while the guests, on their part, could not altogether arrive at the meaning of observations that were couched in the most incomprehensible *patois* that was ever invented. It was 'neither fish, flesh, nor good red herring,' although it was flavoured with the Northumbrian burr, and mixed with a species of Scotch; and the historian of these pages would feel almost as much difficulty in setting down this north-Northumbrian dialect, as he would do were he to attempt to reduce to words the bird-like chatter of the Bosjesmen.

When, for example, the bewigged Mr. Bouncer — 'the laddie wi' the black pow,' as they called him — was addressed as 'Hinny! jist come ben, and crook yer hough on the settle, and het yersen by the chimney-lug,' it was as much by action as by word that he understood an invitation to be seated; though the 'wet yer thrapple wi' a drap o' whuskie, mon!' was easier of comprehension when accompanied with the presentation of the whiskey-horn. In like manner, when Mr. Verdant Green's arrival was announced by the furious barking of the faithful dogs, the apology that 'the camstary breutes of dougs would not steek their clatterin' gabs,' was accepted as an ample explanation, more from the dogs being quieted than from the lucidity of the remark that explained their uproar.

There was one class of lady-labourers, peculiar to that part of the country, who were called Bondagers, — great strapping damsels of three- or four-woman-power, whose occupation it was to draw water, and perform some of the rougher duties attendant upon agricultural pursuits. The sturdy legs of these young ladies were equipped in greaves of leather, which protected them from the cutting attacks of stubble, thistles, and all other lacerating specimens of botany, and their exuberant figures were clad in buskins, and many-coloured garments, that were not long enough to conceal their greaves and clod-hopping boots. Altogether, these young women, when engaged at their ordinary avocations by the side of a spring, formed no unpicturesque subject for the sketcher's pencil, and might have been advantageously transferred to canvas by many an artist who travels to greater distances in search of lesser novelties.

But many peculiar subjects for the pencil might there have been found. One day when they were all going to see the ewe-milking (which of itself would have furnished material for a host of sketches), they suddenly came upon the following scene. Round by the gable of a cottage was seated a shock-headed rustic Absalom, and standing over him was another rustic, who, with a large pair of shears, was acting as an amateur Tonson, and was earnestly engaged in reducing the other's profuse head of hair; an occupation upon which he busied himself with more zeal than discretion. Of this little scene Miss Patty Honeywood forthwith made a memorandum.

For Miss Patty possessed the enviable accomplishment of sketching from nature; and, leaving the beaten track of young-lady figure-artists, who usually limit their efforts to chalk-heads and crayon smudges, she boldy launched into the more difficult, but far more pleasing undertaking of delineating the human form divine from the very life. Mr. Verdant Green found this sketching from nature to be so pretty a pastime, that though unable of himself to produce the feeblest specimen of art, he yet took the greatest delight in watching the facility with which Miss Patty's taper fingers transferred to paper the *vraisemblance* of a pair of sturdy Bondagers, or the miniature reflection of a grand landscape. Happily for him, also, by way of an excuse for bestowing his company upon Miss Patty, he was enabled to be of some use to her in carrying her sketching-block and box of moist water-colours, or in bringing to her water from a neighbouring spring, or in sharpening her pencils. On these occasions Verdant would have preferred their being left to the sole enjoyment of each other's company; but this was not so to be; for they were always favoured with the attendance of at least a third person.

But (at last!) on one happy day, when the bright sunshine was reflected in Miss Patty

Honeywood's bright-beaming face, Mr. Verdant Green found himself wandering forth,

'All in the blue, unclouded weather,'

with his heart's idol, and no third person to intrude upon their duet. The alleged purport of the walk was, that Miss Patty might sketch the ruined church of Lasthope, which was about two miles distant from the Hall. To reach it they had to follow the course of the Swirl, which ran through the Squire's grounds.

The Swirl was a brawling, picturesque stream; at one place narrowing into threads of silver between lichen-covered stones and fragments of rock; at another place flowing on in deep pools —

'Wimpling, dimpling, staying never
Lisping, gurgling, ever going,
Sipping, slipping, ever flowing,
Toying round the polish'd stone;'

fretting 'in rough, shingly shallows wide,' and then 'bickering down the sunny day.' On one day, it might, in places, and with the aid of stepping-stones, be crossed dryshod; and within twenty-four hours it might be swelled by mountain torrents into a river wider than the Thames at Richmond. This sudden growth of the

'Infant of the weeping hills,'

was the reason why the high road was carried over the Swirl by a bridge of ten arches — a circumstance which had greatly excited little Mr. Bouncer's ideas of the ridiculous when he perceived the narrow stream scarcely wide enough to wet the sides of one of the arches of the great bridge that straggled over it, like a railway viaduct over a canal. But, ere his visit to Honeywood Hall had come to an end, the little gentleman had more than once seen the Swirl swollen to its fullest dimensions, and been enabled to recognize the use of the bridge, and the full force of the local expression — 'the waeter is grit'.

As Verdant and Miss Patty made their way along the bank of this most changeable stream, they came upon Mr. Charles Larkyns knee-deep in it, equipped in his wading-boots and fishing dress, and industriously whipping the water for trout. The Swirl was a famous trout-stream, and Mr. Honeywood's coachman was a noted fisherman, and was accustomed to pass many of his nights fishing the stream with a white moth. It appeared that the finny inhabitants of the Swirl were as fond of whitebait as are Cabinet Ministers and London aldermen; for the coachman's deeds of darkness invariably resulted in the production of a fine dish of freshly-caught trout for the breakfast-table.

'It must be hard work,' said Verdant to his friend, as they stopped awhile to watch him; 'it must be hard work to make your way against the stream, and to clamber in and out among the rocks and stones.'

'Not at all hard work,' was Charles Larkyns's reply, 'but play. Play, too, in more senses than one. See! I have just struck a fish. Watch, while I play him. 'The play's the thing!' Wait awhile and you'll see me land him, or I'm much mistaken.'

So they waited awhile and watched this fisherman at play, until he had triumphantly landed his fish, and then they pursued their way.

Miss Patty had great conversational abilities and immense power of small talk, so that Verdant felt quite at ease in her society, and found his natural timidity and quiet bashfulness to be greatly diminished, even if they were not altogether put on one side. They were always such capital friends, and Miss Patty was so kind and thoughtful in making Verdant appear to the best advantage, and in looking over any little *gaucheries* to which his bashfulness might give birth, that it is not to be wondered at if the young gentleman should feel great delight in her society, and should seek for it at every opportunity. In fact, Miss Patty Honeywood was beginning to be quite necessary to Mr. Verdant Green's happy existence. It may be that the young lady was not altogether ignorant of this, but was enabled to read the young man's state of mind, and to judge pretty accurately of his inward feelings, from those minute details of outward evidence which womankind are so quick to mark, and so skilful in tracing to their true source. It may be, also, that the young lady did not choose either to check these feelings or to alter this state of mind — which she certainly ought to have done if she was solicitous for her companion's happiness, and was unable to increase it in the way that he wished.

But, at any rate, with mutual satisfaction for the present, they strolled together along the Swirl's rocky banks, and passing into a large enclosure, they advanced midway through the fields to a spot which seemed a suitable one for Miss Patty's purpose. The brawling stream made a good foreground for the picture, which, on the one side, was shut in by a steep hill rising precipitously from the water's rough bed, and on the other side opened out into a mountainous landscape, having in the near view the ruined church of Lasthope, with the still more ruinous minister's house, a fir plantation, and a rude bridge; with a middle distance of bold, sheep-dotted hills; and for a background the 'sow-backed' Cheviot itself.

Miss Patty had made her outline of this scene, and was preparing to wash it in, when, as her companion came up from the stream with a little tin can of water, he saw, to his equal terror and amazement, a huge bull of the most uninviting aspect stealthily approaching the seated figure of the unconscious young lady. Mr. Verdant Green looked hastily around and at once perceived the danger that menaced his fair friend. It was evident that the bull had come up from the further end of the large enclosure, the while they had been too occupied to observe his stealthy approach. No one was in sight save Charles Larkyns, who was too far off to be of any use. The nearest gate was about a hundred and fifty yards distant; and the bull was so placed that he could overtake them before they would be able to reach it. Overtake them! — yes! But suppose they separated? then, as the brute could not go two ways at once, there would be a chance for one of them to get through the gate in safety. Love, which induces people to take extraordinary steps, prompted Mr. Verdant Green to jump at a conclusion. He determined, with less display but more sincerity than melodramatic heroes, to save Miss Patty, or 'perish in the attempt.'

She was seated on the rising bank altogether ignorant of the presence of danger; and, as Verdant returned to her with the tin can of water, she received him with a happy smile, and a gush of pleasant small talk, which our hero immediately repressed by saying, 'Don't be frightened — there is no danger — but there is a bull coming towards us. Walk quietly to that gate, and keep your face towards him as much as possible, and don't let him see that you are afraid of him. I will take off his attention till you are safe at the gate, and then I can wade through the stream and get out of his reach.'

Miss Patty had at once sprung to her feet, and her smile had changed to a terrified expression. 'Oh, but he will hurt you!' she cried; 'do come with me. It is papa's bull *Roarer*; he is very savage. I can't think what brings him here — he is generally up at the bailiff's. Pray do come; I can take care of myself.'

Miss Patty in her agitation and anxiety had taken hold of Mr. Verdant Green's hand; but, although the young gentleman would at any other time have very willingly allowed her to retain possession of it, on the present occasion he disengaged it from her clasp, and said, 'Pray don't lose time, or it will be too late for both of us. I assure you that I can easily take care of myself. Now do go, pray; quietly, but quickly.' So Miss Patty, with an earnest, searching gaze into her companion's face, did as he bade her, and retreated with her face to the foe.

In a few seconds, however, the object of her movement had dawned upon Mr. Roarer's dull understanding, upon which discovery he set up a bellow of fury, and stamped the ground in very undignified wrath. But, more than this, like a skilful general who has satisfactorily worked out the forty-seventh proposition of the First Book of Euclid, and knows therefrom that the square of the hypothenuse equals both that of the base and perpendicular, he unconsciously commenced the solution of the problem, by making a galloping charge in the direction of the gate to which Miss Patty was hastening. Thereupon, Mr. Verdant Green, perceiving the young lady's peril, deliberately ran towards Mr. Roarer, shouting and brandishing the sketch-book. Mr. Roarer paused in wonder and perplexity. Mr. Verdant Green shouted and advanced; Miss Patty steadily retreated.

After a few moments of indecision Mr. Roarer abandoned his design of pursuing the petticoats, and resolved that the gentleman should be his first victim. Accordingly he sounded his trumpet for the conflict, gave another roar and a stamp, and then ran towards Mr. Verdant Green, who, having picked up a large stone, threw it dexterously into Mr. Roarer's face, which brought that broad-chested gentleman to a stand-still of astonishment and a search for the missile. Of this Mr. Verdant Green took advantage, and made a Parthian retreat. Glancing towards Miss Patty he saw that she was within thirty yards of the gate, and in a minute or two would be in safety — saved through his means!

A bellow from Mr. Roarer's powerful lungs prevented him for the present from pursuing this delightful theme. In another moment the bull charged, and Mr. Verdant Green — braced up, as it were, to energetic proceedings by the screams with which Miss Patty had now begun to shrilly echo Mr. Roarer's deep-mouthed bellowings — waited for his approach, and then, as the bull rushed on him — like a massive rock hurled forward by an avalanche — he leaped aside, nimble as a doubling hare. As he did so, he threw down his wide-awake, which the irate Mr. Roarer forthwith fell upon, and tossed, and tossed, and tore into shreds. By this time, Verdant had reached the bank of the Swirl; but before he could proceed further, the bull was upon him again. Verdant was prepared for this, and had taken off his coat. As the bull dashed heavily towards him, with head bent wickedly to the ground, Verdant again doubled, and, with the dexterity of a matador, threw his coat upon the horns. Blinded by this, Mr. Roarer's headlong career was temporarily checked; and it was three minutes before he had torn to shreds the imaginary body of his enemy; but this three minutes' pause was of very great importance, and in all probability prevented the memoirs of Mr. Verdant Green from coming to an untimely end at this portion of the narrative.

Miss Patty's continued screams had been signals of distress that had not only brought up Charles Larkyns, but four labourers also, who were working in a field within earshot. This *corps de reserve* ran up to the spot with all speed, shouting as they did so, in order to distract Mr. Roarer's attention. By this time Mr. Verdant Green had waded into the water, and was making the best of his way across the Swirl, in order that he might reach the precipitous hill to the right; up this he could scramble and bid defiance to Mr. Roarer. But there is many a slip 'tween cup and lip. Poor Verdant chanced to make a stepping-stone of a treacherous boulder, and fell headlong into the water; and ere he could regain his feet, the bull had plunged with a bellow into the stream, and was within a yard of his prostrate form, when —

When you may imagine Mr. Verdant Green's delight and Miss Patty Honeywood's thankfulness at seeing one of the labourers run into the stream, and strike the bull a heavy stroke with a sharp hoe, the pain of which wound caused Mr. Roarer to suddenly wheel round and engage with his new adversary, who followed up his advantage, and cut into his enemy with might and main. Then Charles Larkyns and the other three labourers came up, and the bull was prevented from doing an injury to any one until a farm-servant had arrived upon the scene with a strong halter, when Mr. Roarer, somewhat spent with wrath, and suffering from considerable depression of animal spirits, was conducted to the obscure retirement and littered ease of the bull-house.

This little adventure has been recorded here, inasmuch as from it was forged, by the hand of Cupid, a golden link in our hero's chain of fate; for to this occurrence Miss Patty attached no slight importance. She exalted Mr. Verdant Green's conduct on this occasion into an act of heroism worthy to be ranked with far more notable deeds of valour. She looked upon him as a Bayard who had chivalrously risked his life in the cause of — love, was it? or only of — a lady. Her gratitude, she considered, ought to be very great to one who had, at so great a venture, preserved her from so horrible a death. For that she would have been dreadfully gored, and would have lost her life, if she had not been rescued by Mr. Verdant Green, Miss Patty had most fully and unalterably decided — which, certainly, might have been the case.

At any rate, our hero had no reason to regret that portion of his life's drama in which Mr. Roarer had made his appearance.

3

Mr. Verdant Green Studies ye Manners and Customs of ye Natyves

Miss Patty Honeywood was not only distinguished for unlimited powers of conversation, but was also equally famous for her equestrian abilities. She and her sister were the first horsewomen in that part of the county; and, if their father had permitted, they would have been delighted to ride to hounds, and to cross country with the foremost flight, for they had pluck enough for anything. They had such light hands and good seats, and in every respect rode so well, that, as a matter of course, they looked well — never better, perhaps, than — when on horseback. Their bright, happy faces — which were far more beautiful in their piquant irregularities of feature, and gave one far more pleasure in the contemplation than if they had been moulded in the coldly chiselled forms of classic beauty — appeared with no diminution of charms, when set off by their pretty felt riding-hats; and their full, firm, and well-rounded figures were seen to the greatest advantage when clad in the graceful dress that passes by the name of a riding-habit.

Every morning, after breakfast, the two young ladies were accustomed to visit the stables, where they had interviews with their respective steeds — steeds and mistresses appearing to be equally gratified thereby. It is perhaps needless to state that during Mr. Verdant Green's sojourn at Honeywood Hall, Miss Patty's stable calls were generally made in his company.

Such rides as they took in those happy days — wild, pic-nic sort of rides, over country equally as wild and removed from formality — rides by duets and rides in duodecimos; sometimes a solitary couple or two; sometimes a round dozen of them, scampering and racing over hill and heather, with startled grouse and black-cock skirring up from under the very hoofs of the equally startled horses — rides by tumbling streams, like the Swirl — splashing through them, with pulled-up or draggled habits — then cantering on 'over bank, bush, and scaur,' like so many fair Ellens and young Lochinvars — clambering up very precipices, and creeping down break-neck hills — laughing and talking, and singing, and whistling, and even (so far as Mr. Bouncer was concerned) blowing cows' horns! What vagabond, rollicking rides were those! What a healthy contrast to the necessarily formal, groom-attended canter on Society's Rotten Row!

A legion of dogs accompanied them on these occasions; a miscellaneous pack composed of Masters Huz and Buz (in great spirits at finding themselves in such capital quarters), a black Newfoundland (answering to the name of 'Blackie'), a couple of setters (with titles from the heathen mythology — 'Juno' and 'Flora'), a ridiculous-looking, bandy-legged otter-hound (called 'Gripper'), a wiry, rat-catching terrier ('Nipper'), and two silky-haired, long-backed, short-legged, sharp-nosed, bright-eyed, pepper-and-salt Skye-terriers, who respectively answered to the names of 'Whisky' and 'Toddy,' and were the property of the Misses Honey-wood. The lordly shepherds' dogs, whom they encountered on their journeys, would have nothing to do with such a medley of unruly scamps, but turned from their overtures of friendship with patrician disdain. They routed up rabbits; they turned out hedgehogs; and, at their approach, they made the game fly with a WHIR-R-R-R-R-R arranged as a *diminuendo*.

These free-and-easy equestrian expeditions were not only agreeable to Mr. Verdant Green's feelings, but they were also useful to him as so many lessons of horsemanship, and so greatly advanced him in the practice of that noble science, that the admiring Squire one day said to him — 'I'll tell you what, Verdant! before we've done with you, we shall make you ride like a Shafto!' At which high eulogium Mr. Verdant Green blushed, and made an inward resolution that, as soon as he had returned home, he would subscribe to the Warwickshire hounds, and make his appearance in the field.

On Sundays the Honeywood party usually rode and drove to the church of a small market-town, some seven or eight miles distant. If it was a wet day, they walked to the ruined church of Lasthope — the place Miss Patty was sketching when disturbed by Mr. Roarer. Lasthope was in lay hands; and its lay rector, who lived far away, had so little care for the edifice, or the proper conduct of divine service, that he allowed the one to continue in its ruins, and suffered the other to be got through anyhow or not at all — just as it happened. Clergymen were engaged to perform the service (there was but one each day) at the lowest price of the clerical market. Occasionally it was announced, in the vernacular of the district, that there would be no church, 'because the priest had gone for the sea-bathing,' or because the waters were out, and the priest could not get across. As a matter of course, in consequence of the uncertainty of finding any one to perform the service when they had got to church, and of the slovenly way in which the service was scrambled through when they had got a clergyman there, the congregation generally preferred attending the large Presbyterian meeting-house, which was about two miles from Lasthope. Here, at any rate, they met with the reverse of coldness in the conduct of the service.

Mr. Verdant Green and his male friends strayed there one Sunday for curiosity's sake, and found a minister of indefatigable eloquence and enviable power of lungs, who had arrived at such a pitch of heat, from the combined effects of the weather and his own exertions, that in the very middle of his discourse — and literally in the heat of it — he paused to divest himself of his gown, heavily braided with serge and velvet, and, hanging it over the side of the pulpit ('the pilput,' his congregation called it), mopped his head with his handkerchief, and then pursued his theme like a giant refreshed. At this stage in the proceedings, little Mr. Bouncer became in a high state of pleasurable excitement, from the expectation that the minister would next divest himself of his coat, and would struggle through the rest of his argument in his shirt-sleeves; but Mr. Bouncer's improper wishes were not gratified.

The sermon was so extremely metaphorical, was founded on such abstruse passages, and was delivered in so broad a dialect, that it was *caviare* to Mr. Verdant Green and his friends; but it seemed to be far otherwise with the attentive and crowded congregation, who relieved their minister at intervals by loud bursts of singing, that were impressive from their fervency though not particularly harmonious to a delicately-musical ear. Near to the close of the service there was a collection, which induced Mr. Bouncer to whisper to Verdant — as an axiom deduced from his long experience — that 'you never come to a strange place, but what you are sure to drop in for a collection;' but, on finding that it was a weekly offering, and that no one was expected to give more than a copper, the little gentleman relented, and cheerfully dropped a piece of silver into the wooden box. It was astonishing to see the throngs of people, that, in so thinly inhabited a district, could be assembled at this meeting-house. Though it seemed almost incredible to our midland-county friends, yet not a few of these poor, simple, earnest-minded people would walk from a distance of fifteen miles, starting at an early hour, coming by easy stages, and bringing with them their dinner, so as to enable them to stay for the afternoon service.

On the Sunday mornings the red cloaks and grey plaids of these pious men and women might be seen dotting the green hillsides, and slowly moving towards the gaunt and grim red brick meeting-house. And around it, on great occasions, were tents pitched for the between-service accommodation of the worshippers.

Both they and it contrasted, in every way, with the ruined church of Lasthope, whose worship seemed also to have gone to ruin with the uncared-for edifice. Its aisles had tumbled down, and their material had been rudely built up within the arches of the nave. The church was thus converted into the non-ecclesiastical form of a parallelogram, and was fitted up with the very rudest and ugliest of deal enclosures, which were dignified with the name of pews, but ought to have been termed pens.

During the time of Mr. Verdant Green's visit, the service at this ecclesiastical ruin was performed by a clergyman who had apparently been selected for the duty from his harmonious resemblance to the place; for he also was an ecclesiastical ruin — a schoolmaster in holy orders, who, having to slave hard all through the working-days of the week, had to work still harder on the day of rest. For, first, the Ruin had to ride his stumbling old pony a distance of twelve miles (and twelve *such* miles!) to Lasthope, where he stabled it (bringing the feed of corn in his pocket, and leading it to drink at the Swirl) in the dilapidated stable of the tumbled-down rectory-house. Then he had to get through the morning service without any loss of time, to enable him to ride eight miles in another direction (eating his sandwich dinner as he went along), where he had to take the afternoon duty and occasional services at a second church. When this was done, he might find his way home as well as he could, and enjoy with his family as much of the day of rest as he had leisure and strength for. The stipend that the Ruin received for his labours was greatly below the wages given to a butler by the lay rector, who pocketed a very nice income by this respectable transaction. But the Butler was a stately edifice in perfect repair, both outside and in, so far as clothes and food went; and the Parson was an ill-conditioned Ruin left to moulder away in an obscure situation, without even the ivy of luxuriance to make him graceful and picturesque.

Mr. Honeywood's family were the only 'respectable' persons who occasionally attended the Ruin's ministrations in Lasthope church. The other people who made up the scanty congregation were old Andrew Graham and his children, and a few of the poorer sort of Honeybourn. They all brought their dogs with them as a matter of course. On entering the church the men hung up their bonnets on a row of pegs provided for that purpose, and fixed, as an ecclesiastical ornament, along the western wall of the church. They then took their places in their pens, accompanied by their dogs, who usually behaved with remarkable propriety, and, during the sermon, set their masters an example of watchfulness. On one occasion the proceedings were interrupted by a rat hunt; the dogs gave tongue, and leaped the pews in the excitement of the chase — their masters followed them and laid about them with their sticks — and when with difficulty order had been restored, the service was proceeded with. It must be confessed that Mr. Bouncer was so badly disposed as to wish for a repetition of this scene; but (happily) he was disappointed.

The choir of Lasthope Church was centred in the person of the clerk, who apparently sang tunes of his own composing, in which the congregation joined at their discretion, though usually to different airs. The result was a discordant struggle, through which the clerk bravely maintained his own until he had exhausted himself, when he shut up his book and sat down, and the congregation had to shut up also. During the singing the intelligence of the dogs was displayed in their giving a stifled utterance to howls of anguish, which were repeated *ad libitum* throughout the hymn; but as this was a customary proceeding it attracted no attention, unless a dog expressed his sufferings more loudly than was wont, when he received a clout from his master's staff that silenced him, and sent him under the pew-seat, as to a species of ecclesiastical St. Helena.

Such was Lasthope Church, its Ruin, and its service; and, as may be imagined from these notes which the veracious historian has thought fit to chronicle, Mr. Verdant Green found that his Sundays in Northumberland produced as much novelty as the week-days.

4

Mr. Verdant Green Endeavours to Say Snip to Someone's Snap

There was a gate in the kitchen-garden of Honeywood Hall, that led into an orchard; and in this orchard there was a certain apple-tree that had assumed one of those peculiarities of form to which the children of Pomona are addicted. After growing upright for about a foot and a half, it had suddenly shot out at right angles, with a gentle upward slope for a length of between three and four feet, and had then again struck up into the perpendicular. It thus formed a natural orchard seat, capable of holding two persons comfortably — provided that they regarded a close proximity as comfortable sitting.

One day Miss Patty directed Verdant's attention to this vagary of nature. 'This is one of my favourite haunts,' she said. 'I often steal here on a hot day with some work or a book. You see this upper branch makes quite a little table, and I can rest my book upon it. It is so pleasant to be under the shade here, with the fruit or blossoms over one's head; and it is so snug and retired, and out of the way of every one.'

'It *is* very snug — and very retired,' said Mr. Verdant Green; and he thought that now would be the very time to put in execution a project that had for some days past been haunting his brain.

'When Kitty and I,' said Miss Patty, 'have any secrets we come here and tell them to each other while we sit at our work. No one can hear what we say; and we are quite snug all to ourselves.'

Very odd, thought Verdant, that they should fix on this particular spot for confidential communications, and take the trouble to come here to make them, when they could do so in their own rooms at the house. And yet it isn't such a bad spot either.

'Try how comfortable a seat it is!' said Miss Patty.

Mr. Verdant Green began to feel hot. He sat down, however, and tested the comforts of the seat, much in the same way as he would try the spring of a lounging chair, and apparently with a like result, for he said, 'Yes, it *is* very comfortable — very comfortable indeed.'

'I thought you'd like it,' said Miss Patty; 'and you see how nicely the branches droop all round: they make it quite an arbour. If

Kitty had been here with me I think you would have had some trouble to have found us.'

'I think I should; it is quite a place to hide in,' said Verdant. But the young lady and gentleman must have been speaking with the spirit of ostriches, and have imagined that, when they had hidden their heads, they had altogether concealed themselves from observation; for the branches of the apple-tree only drooped low enough to conceal the upper part of their figures, and left the rest exposed to view. 'Won't you sit down, also?' asked Verdant, with a gasp and a sensation in his head as though he had been drinking champagne too freely.

'I'm afraid there's scarcely room for me,' pleaded Miss Patty.

'Oh yes, there is, indeed! pray sit down.'

So she sat down on the lower part of the trunk. Mr. Verdant Green glanced rapidly round and perceived that they were quite alone, and partly shrouded from view. The following highly interesting conversation then took place.

He. 'Won't you change places with me? you'll slip off.'

She. 'No — I think I can manage.'

He. 'But you can come closer.'

She. 'Thanks.' (*She comes closer.*)

He. 'Isn't that more comfortable?'

She. 'Yes — very much.'

He. (*Very hot, and not knowing what to say*) — 'I — I think you'll slip!'

She. 'Oh no! it's very comfortable indeed.' (That is to say — thinks Mr. Verdant Green — that sitting BY ME is very comfortable. Hurrah!)

She. 'It's very hot, don't you think?'

He. 'How very odd! I was just thinking the same.'

She. 'I think I shall take my hat off — it is so warm. Dear me! how stupid! — the strings are in a knot.'

He. 'Let me see if I can untie them for you.'

She. 'Thanks! no! I can manage.' (*But she cannot.*)

He. 'You'd better let me try! now do!'

She. 'Oh, thanks! but I'm sorry you should have the trouble.'

He. 'No trouble at all. Quite a pleasure.'

In a very hot condition of mind and fingers, Mr. Verdant Green then endeavoured to release the strings from their entanglement. But all in vain: he tugged, and pulled, and only made matters worse. Once or twice in the struggle his hands touched Miss Patty's chin; and no highly-charged electrical machine could have imparted a shock greater than that tingling sensation of pleasure which Mr. Verdant Green experienced when his fingers, for the fraction of a second, touched Miss Patty's soft dimpled chin. Then there was her beautiful neck, so white, and with such blue veins! he had an irresistible desire to stroke it for its very smoothness — as one loves to feel the polish of marble, or the glaze of wedding cards — instead of employing his hands in fumbling at the brown ribands, whose knots became more complicated than ever. Then there was her happy rosy face, so close to which his own was brought; and her bright, laughing, hazel eyes, in which, as he timidly looked up, he saw little daguerreotypes of himself. Would that he could retain such a photographer by his side through life! Miss

Bouncer's camera was as nothing compared with the *camera lucida* of those clear eyes, that shone upon him so truthfully, and mirrored for him such pretty pictures. And what with these eyes, and the face, and the chin, and the neck, Mr. Verdant Green was brought into such an irretrievable state of mental excitement that he was perfectly unable to render Miss Patty the service he had proffered. But, more than that, he as yet lacked sufficient courage to carry out his darling project.

At length Miss Patty herself untied the rebellious knot, and took off her hat. The highly interesting conversation was then resumed.

She. 'What a frightful state my hair is in!' (*Loops up an escaped lock.*) 'You must think me so untidy. But out in the country, and in a place like this where no one sees us, it makes one careless of appearance.'

He. 'I like 'a sweet neglect,' especially in — in some people; it suits them so well. I — 'pon my word, it's very hot!'

She. 'But how much hotter it must be from under the shade. It is so pleasant here. It seems so dreamlike to sit among the shadows and look out upon the bright landscape.'

He. 'It *is* — very jolly — soothing, at least!' (*A pause.*) 'I think you'll slip. Do you know, I think it will be safer if you will let me' (*here his courage fails him. He endeavours to say* put my arm round your waist, *but his tongue refuses to speak the words; so he substitutes*) 'change places with you.'

She. (*Rises, with a look of amused vexation.*) 'Certainly! If you so particularly wish it.' (*They change places.*) 'Now, you see, you have lost by the change. You are too tall for that end of the seat, and it did very nicely for a little body like me.'

He. (*With a thrill of delight and a sudden burst of strategy.*) 'I can hold on to this branch, if my arm will not inconvenience you.'

She. 'Oh no! not particularly:' (*he passes his right arm behind her, and takes hold of a bough:*) 'but I should think it's not very comfortable for you.'

He. 'I couldn't be more comfortable, I'm sure.' (*Nearly slips off the tree, and doubles up his legs into an unpicturesque attitude highly suggestive of misery. — A pause*) 'And do you tell your secrets here?'

She. 'My secrets? Oh, I see — you mean, with Kitty. Oh, yes! if this tree could talk, it would be able to tell such dreadful stories.'

He. 'I wonder if it could tell any dreadful stories of — *me?*'

She. 'Of you? Oh, no! Why should it? We are only severe on those we dislike.'

He. 'Then you don't dislike me?'

She. 'No! — why should we?'

He. 'Well — I don't know — but I thought you might. Well, I'm glad of that — I'm *very* glad of that. 'Pon my word, it's *very* hot! don't you think so?'

She. 'Yes! I'm burning. But I don't think we should find a cooler place.' (*Does not evince any symptoms of moving.*)

He. 'Well, p'raps we shouldn't.' (*A pause.*) 'Do you know that I'm very glad you don't dislike me; because, it wouldn't have been pleasant to be disliked by you, would it?'

She. 'Well — of course, I can't tell. It depends upon one's own feelings.'

He. 'Then you don't dislike me?'

She. 'Oh dear, no! why should I?'

He. 'And if you don't dislike me, you must like me?'

She. 'Yes — at least — yes, I suppose so.'

At this stage of the proceedings, the arm that Mr. Verdant Green had passed behind Miss Patty thrilled with such a peculiar sensation that his hand slipped down the bough, and the arm consequently came against Miss Patty's waist, where it rested. The necessity for saying something, the wish to make that something the something that was bursting his heart and brain, and the dread of letting it escape his lips — these three varied and mingled sensations so distracted poor Mr. Verdant Green's mind, that he was no more conscious of what he was giving utterance to than if he had been talking in a dream. But there was Miss Patty by his side — a very tangible and delightful reality — playing (somewhat nervously) with those rebellious strings of her hat, which loosely hung in her hand, while the dappled shadows flickered on the waving masses of her rich brown hair, — so something must be said; and, if it should lead to *the* something, why, so much the better.

Returning, therefore, to the subject of like and dislike, Mr. Verdant Green managed to say, in a choking, faltering tone, 'I wonder how much you like me — very much?'

She. 'Oh, I couldn't tell — how should I? What strange questions you ask! You saved my life; so, of course, I am very, very grateful; and I hope I shall always be your friend.'

He. 'Yes, I hope so indeed — always — and something more. Do you hope the same?'

She. 'What *do* you mean? Hadn't we better go back to the house?'

He. 'Not just yet — it's so cool here — at least, not cool exactly, but hot — pleasanter, that is — much pleasanter here. *You* said so, you know, a little while since. Don't mind me; I always feel hot when — when I'm out of doors.'

She. 'Then we'd better go indoors.'

He. 'Pray don't — not yet — do stop a little longer.'

And the hand that had been on the bough of the tree, timidly seized Miss Patty's arm, and then naturally, but very gently, fell upon her waist. A thrill shot through Mr. Verdant Green, like an electric flash, and, after traversing from his head to his heels, probably passed out safely at his boots — for it did him no harm, but, on the contrary, made him feel all the better.

'But,' said the young lady, as she felt the hand upon her waist — not that she was really displeased at the proceeding, but perhaps she thought it best, under the circumstances, to say something that should have the resemblance of a veto — 'but it is not necessary to hold me a prisoner.'

'It's *you* that hold *me* a prisoner!' said Mr. Verdant Green, with a sudden burst of enthusiasm and blushes, and a great stress upon the pronouns.

'Now you are talking nonsense, and, if so, I must go!' said Miss Patty. And she also blushed; perhaps it was from the heat. But she removed Mr. Verdant Green's hand from her waist, and he was much too frightened to replace it.

'Oh! *do* stay a little!' gasped the young gentleman, with an awkward sensation of want of employment for his hands. 'You said that secrets were told here. I don't want to talk nonsense; I don't indeed; but the truth. *I've* a secret to tell you. Should you like to hear it?'

'Oh yes!' laughed Miss Patty. 'I like to hear secrets.'

Now, how very absurd it was in Mr. Verdant Green wasting time in beating about the bush in this ridiculously timid way! Why could he not at once boldly secure his bird by a straightforward shot? She did not fly out of his range — did she? And yet, here he was making himself unnecessarily hot and uncomfortable, when he might, by taking it coolly, have been at his ease in a moment. What a foolish young man! Nay, he still further lost time and evaded his purpose, by saying once again to Miss Patty — instead of immediately replying to her observation — ''Pon my word, it's uncommonly hot! don't you think so?'

Upon which Miss Patty replied, with some little chagrin, 'And was that your secret?' If she had lived in the Elizabethan era she could have adjured him with a 'Marry, come up!' which would have brought him to the point without any further trouble; but living in a Victorian age, she could do no more than say what she did, and leave the rest of her meaning to the language of the eyes.

'Don't laugh at me!' urged the bashful and weak-minded young man; 'don't laugh at me!

If you only knew what I feel when you laugh at me, you'd — '

'Cry, I dare say!' said Miss Patty, cutting him short with a merry smile, and (it must be confessed) a most wickedly roguish expression about those bright flashing hazel eyes of hers. 'Now, you haven't told me this wonderful secret!'

'Why,' said Mr. Verdant Green, slowly and deliberately — feeling that his time was coming on, and cowardly anxious still to fight off the fatal words — 'you said that you didn't dislike me; and, in fact, that you liked me very much; and' —

But here Miss Patty cut him short again. She turned sharply round upon him, with those bright eyes and that merry face, and said, 'Oh! how *can* you say so? I never said anything of the sort!'

'Well,' said Mr. Verdant Green, who was now desperate, and mentally prepared to take the dreaded plunge into that throbbing sea that beats upon the strand of matrimony, 'whether *you* like *me* very much or not, *I* like *you* very much! — very much indeed! Ever since I saw you, since last Christmas, I've — I've liked you — very much indeed.'

Mr. Verdant Green, in a very hot and excited state, had, while he was speaking, timidly brought his hand once more to Miss

Patty's waist; and she did not interfere with its position. In fact, she was bending down her head, and was gazing intently on another knot that she had wilfully made in her hat-strings; and she was working so violently at that occupation of untying the knot, that very probably she might not have been aware of the situation of Mr. Verdant Green's hand. At any rate, her own hands were too much busied to suffer her to interfere with his.

At last the climax had arrived. Mr. Verdant Green had screwed his courage to the sticking point, and had resolved to tell the secret of his love. He had got to the very edge of the precipice, and was on the point of jumping over head and ears into the stream of his destiny, and of bursting into any excited form of words that should make known his affection and his designs, when — when a vile perfume of tobacco, a sudden barking rush of Huz and Buz, and the horrid voice of little Mr. Bouncer, dispelled the bright vision, dispersed his ideas, and prevented the fulfilment of his purpose.

'Holloa, Giglamps!' roared the little gentleman, as he removed a short pipe from his mouth, and expelled an ascending curl of smoke; 'I've been looking for you everywhere! Here we are, — as Hamlet's uncle said, — all in the horchard! I hope he's not been pouring poison in *your* ear, Miss Honeywood; he looks rather guilty. The Mum — I mean your mother — sent me to find you. The luncheon's been on the table more than an hour!'

Luckily for Mr. Verdant Green and Miss Patty Honeywood, little Mr. Bouncer rattled on without waiting for any reply to his observations, and thus enabled the young lady to somewhat recover her presence of mind, and to effect a hasty retreat from under the apple-tree, and through the garden gate.

'I say, old feller,' said Mr. Bouncer, as he criticized Mr. Verdant Green's countenance over the bowl of his pipe, 'you look rather in a stew! What's up? My gum!' cried the little gentleman, as an idea of the truth suddenly flashed upon him; 'you don't mean to say you've been doing the spooney — what you call making love — have you?'

'Oh!' groaned the person addressed, as he followed out the train of his own ideas; 'if you *had* but have come five minutes later — or not at all! It's most provoking!'

'Well, you're a grateful bird, I don't think!' said Mr. Bouncer. 'Cut after her into luncheon, and have it out over the cold mutton and pickles!'

'Oh no!' responded the luckless lover; 'I can't eat — especially before the others! I mean — I couldn't talk to her before the others. Oh! I don't know what I'm saying.'

'Well, I don't think you do, old feller!' said Mr. Bouncer, puffing away at his pipe. 'I'm sorry I was in the road, though! because, though I fight shy of those sort of things myself, yet I don't want to interfere with the little weaknesses of other folks. But come and have a pipe, old feller, and we'll talk matters over, and see what pips are on the cards, and what's the state of the game.'

Now, a pipe was Mr. Bouncer's panacea for every kind of indisposition, both mental and bodily.

5

Mr. Verdant Green Meets with the Green-eyed Monster

Mention had frequently been made by the members of the Honeywood family, but more especially by Miss Patty, of a cousin — a male cousin — to whom they all seemed to be exceedingly partial — far more partial, as Mr. Verdant Green thought, with regard to Miss Patty, than he would have wished her to have been. This cousin was Mr. Frank Delaval, a son of their father's sister. According to their description, he possessed good looks, and an equivalently good fortune, with all sorts of accomplishments, both useful and ornamental; and was, in short (in their eyes at least), a very admirable Crichton of the nineteenth century.

Mr. Verdant Green had heard from Miss Patty so much of her cousin Frank, and of the pleasure they were anticipating from a visit he had promised shortly to make to them, that he had at length begun to suspect that the young lady's maiden meditations were not altogether 'fancy free,' and that her thoughts dwelt upon this handsome cousin far more than was palatable to Mr. Verdant Green's feelings. In the most unreasonable manner, therefore, he conceived a violent antipathy to Mr. Frank Delaval, even before he had set eyes upon him, and considered that the Honeywood family had, one and all, greatly overrated him. But these suppositions and suspicions made him doubly anxious to come to an understanding with Miss Patty before the arrival of the dreaded Adonis; and it was this thought that had helped to nerve him through the terrors of the orchard scene, and which, but for Mr. Bouncer's *malapropos* intrusion, would have brought things to a crisis.

However, after he had had a talk with Mr. Bouncer, and had been fortified by that little gentleman's pithy admonitions to 'go in and win,' and to 'strike while the iron's hot,' and that 'faint heart never won a nice young 'ooman,' he determined to seek out Miss Patty at once, and bring to an end their unfinished conversation. For this purpose he returned to the hall, where he found a great commotion, and a carriage at the door; and out of the carriage jumped a handsome young man, with a black moustache, who ran up to the open hall-door (where Miss Patty was standing with her sister), seized Miss Kitty by the hand, and placed his moustache under her nose, and then seized Miss Patty by *her* hand, and removed the moustache to beneath *her* nose! And all this unblushingly and as a matter of course, out in the sunshine, and before the servants! Mr. Verdant Green retreated without having been seen, and, plunging into the shrubbery, told his woes to the evergreens, and while he listened to

'The dry-tongued laurel's pattering talk,'

he thought, 'It is as I feared! I am nothing more to her than a simple friend.' Though, why he so morosely arrived at this idea it would be hard to say. Perhaps other jealous lovers have been similarly unreasonable and unreasoning in their conclusions, and, of their own accord, run to the dark side of the cloud, when they might have pleasantly remained within its silver lining.

But when Frank Delaval had been seen, and heard, and made acquaintance with, Verdant, who was much too simple-hearted to dislike any one without just grounds for so doing, entered (even after half an hour's knowledge) into the band of his admirers; and that same evening, in the drawing-room, while Miss Kitty was playing one of Schulhoff's mazurkas, with her moustached cousin standing by her side, and turning over the music-leaves, Verdant privately declared, over a chessboard, to Miss Patty, that Mr. Frank Delaval was the handsomest and most delightful man he had ever met. And when Miss Patty's eyes sparkled at this proof of his truth and disinterestedness, Verdant mistook the bright signals; and further misconstruing the cause why (as they continued to speak of her cousin) she made a most egregious blunder, that caused her opponent to pronounce the word 'Mated!' he regarded it as a fatal omen, more especially as Mr. Frank came to her side at that very moment; and when the young lady laughed, and said, 'What a goose I am! whatever could I have been thinking of?' he thought within himself (persisting in his illogical and perverse conclusions), 'It is very plain what she is thinking about! I was afraid that she loved him, and now I know it.' So he put up the chess-men, while she went to the piano with her cousin; and he even wished that Mr. Bouncer had interrupted their apple-tree conversation at its commencement; but was thankful to him for coming in time to save him from the pain of being rejected in favour of another. Then, in five minutes, he changed his mind, and had decided that it would have spared him much misery if he could have heard his fate from his Patty's own lips. Then he wished that he had never come to Northumberland at all, and began to think how he should spend his time in the purgatory that Honeywood Hall would now be to him.

When they separated for the night, HE again placed his moustache beneath HER nose. Mr. Verdant Green turned away his head at such a sickly exhibition. It was a presumption upon cousinship. Charles Larkyns did not kiss her; and he was equally as much her cousin as Frank Delaval.

And yet, when the young men went into the back kitchen for a pipe and a chat before going to bed, Verdant was so delighted with that handsome cousin Frank, that he thought, 'If I was a girl, I should think as *she* does.'

'And why should she not love him?' meditated the poor fellow, when he was lying awake in his bed that self-same night, rendered sleepless by the pain of his new wound; 'why should she not love him? how could she do otherwise? thrown together as they have been from children — speaking to each other as 'Patty' and 'Frank' — kissing each other — and being as brother and sister. Would that they were so! How he kept near her all the evening — coming to her even when she was playing chess with *me*, then singing with her, and playing her accompaniments. She said that no one could play her accompaniments like *he* could — he had such good taste, and such a firm, delicate touch. Then, when they talked about sketching, she said how she had missed him, and that she had been reserving the view from Brankham Law, in order that they might sketch it together. Then he showed her his last drawings — and they were beautiful. What can I do against this?' groaned poor Verdant, from under the bedclothes; 'he has accomplishments, and I have none; he has good looks, and I haven't; he has a moustache and a pair of whiskers, — and I have only a pair of spectacles! I cannot shine in society, and win admiration, like he does; I have nothing to offer her but my love. Lucky fellow! he is worthier of her than I am — and I hope they will be very happy.' At which thought, Verdant felt highly the reverse, and went off into dismal dreams.

In the morning, when Miss Patty and her cousin were setting out for the hill called Brankham Law, Verdant, who had retreated to a garden-seat beneath a fine old cedar, was roused from a very abstracted perusal of 'The Dream of Fair Women,' by the apparition of one who, in his eyes, was fairer than them all. 'I have been searching for you everywhere,' said Miss Patty. 'Mamma said that you were not riding with the others, so I knew that you must be somewhere about. I think I shall lock up my *Tennyson*, if it takes you so much out of our society. Won't you come up Brankham Law with Frank and me?'

'Willingly if you wish it,' answered Verdant, though with an unwilling air; 'but of what use can I be? — Othello's occupation is gone. Your cousin can fill my place much better than if I were there.'

'How very ungrateful you are!' said Miss Patty; 'you really deserve a good scolding! I allow you to watch me when I am painting, in order that you may gain a lesson, and just when you are beginning to learn something, then you give up. But, at any rate, take Frank for your master, and come and watch *him*; he *can* draw. If you were to go to any of the great men to have a lesson of them, all that they would do would be to paint before you, and leave you to look on and pick up what knowledge you could. I know that *I* cannot draw anything worth looking at — '

'Indeed, but — '

'But Frank,' continued Miss Patty, who was going at too great a pace to be stopped, 'but Frank is as good as many masters that you would meet with; so it will be an advantage to you to come and look over him.'

'I think I should prefer to look over you.'

'Now you are paying compliments, and I don't like them. But, if you will come, you will really be useful. You see I am mercenary in my wishes, after all. Here is Frank with a load of sketching materials; won't you take pity on him, and relieve him of my share of his burden?'

If I could take *you* off his hands, thought Verdant, I should be better pleased. But Miss Patty won the day; and Verdant took possession of her sketching-block and drawing materials, and set off with them to Brankham Law.

Frank Delaval was a yachtsman, and owner of the *Fleur-de-lys*, a cutter yacht, of fifty tons. Besides being inclined to amateur nautical pursuits, he was also partial to an amateur nautical costume; and he further dressed the character of a yachtsman by slinging round him his telescope, which was protected from storms and salt water by a leathern case. This telescope was, in a moment, uncased and brought to bear upon everybody and everything, at every opportunity, in proper nautical fashion, being used by him for distant objects as other people would use an eyeglass for nearer things. And no sooner had they arrived at the grassy *plateau* that marked the summit of Brankham Law, than the telescope was unslung, and its proprietor swept the horizon — for there was a distant view of the ocean — in search of the *Fleur-de-lys*.

'I am afraid,' he said, 'that we shall not be able to make her out; the distance is almost too great to distinguish her from other vessels, although the whiteness of her sails would assist us to a recognition. If the skipper got under way at the hour I told him, he ought about this time to be rounding the headland that you see stretching out yonder.'

'I think I see a white sail in that direction,' said Miss Patty, as she shaded her eyes with her hand, and looked out earnestly in the required quarter.

'My dear Patty,' laughed her cousin, 'if you knew anything of nautical matters, you would see that it was not a cutter yacht, for she has more than one mast; though, certainly, as you saw her, she seemed to have but one, for she was just coming about, and was in stays.'

'In stays!' exclaimed Miss Patty; 'why what singular expressions you sailors have!'

'Oh yes!' said Frank Delaval, 'and some vessels have waists — like young ladies. But now I think I see the *Fleur-de-lys*! that gaff tops'l yard was never carried by a coasting vessel. To be sure it is! the skipper knows how to handle her; and, if the breeze holds, she will soon reach her port. Come and have a look at her, Patty, while I rest the glass for you.' So he balanced it on his shoulder, while Miss Patty looked through it with her one eye, and placed her fingers upon the other — after the manner of young ladies when they look through a telescope; and then burst into such animated, but not thoughtful observations, as 'Oh! I can see it quite plainly. Oh! it is rolling about so! Oh! there are two little men in it! Oh! one of them's pulling a rope! Oh! it all seems to be brought so near!' as if there had been some doubt on the matter, and she had expected the telescope to make things invisible. Miss Patty was quite in childish delight at watching the *Fleur-de-lys'* movements, and seemed to forget all about the proposed sketch, although Mr. Verdant Green had found her a comfortable rock seat, and had placed her drawing materials ready for use.

'How happy and confiding they are!' he thought, as he gazed upon them thus standing together; 'they seem to be made for each other. He is far more fitted for her than I am. I wonder if I shall ever see them after they are — married. *I* shall never be married.' And, after this morbid fashion, the young gentleman took a melancholy pleasure in arranging his future.

It was about this time that the divine

afflatus — which had lain almost dormant since his boyish 'Address to the Moon' — was again manifested in him by the production of numberless poetical effusions, in which his own poignant anguish and Miss Patty's incomparable attractions were brought forward in verses of various degrees of mediocrity. They were also equally varied in their style and treatment; one being written in a fierce and gloomy Byronic strain, while another followed the lighter childish style of Wordsworth. To this latter class, perhaps, belonged the following lines, which, having accidentally fallen into the hands of Mr. Bouncer, were pronounced by him to be 'no end good! first-rate fun!' for the little gentleman put a highly erroneous construction upon them, and, to the great laceration of the author's feelings, imagined them to be altogether of a comic tendency. But, when Mr. Verdant Green wrote them, he probably thought that 'deep meaning lieth oft in childish play':—

> 'Pretty Patty Honeywood,
> Fresh, and fair, and plump,
> Into your affections
> I should like to jump!
> Into your good graces
> I should like to steal;

That you lov'd me truly
I should like to feel.

'Pretty Patty Honeywood,
You can little know
How my sea of passion
Unto you doth flow;
How it ever hastens,
With a swelling tide,
To its strand of happiness
At thy darling side.

'Pretty Patty Honeywood,
Would that you and I
Could ask the surpliced parson
Our wedding knot to tie!
Oh! my life of sunshine
Then would be begun,
Pretty Patty Honeywood,
When you and I were one.'

But by far his greatest poetical achievement
was his 'Legend of the Fair Margaret,' written
in Spenserian metre, and commenced at this
period of his career, though never completed.
The plot was of the most dismal and intricate
kind. The Fair Margaret was beloved by two
young men, one of whom (Sir Frankerico)
was dark, and (necessarily, therefore) as badly
disposed a young man as you would desire to

keep out of your family circle, and the other (Sir Verdour) was light, and (consequently) as mild and amiable as any given number of maiden aunts could wish. As a matter of course, therefore, the Fair Margaret perversely preferred the dark Sir Frankerico, who had poisoned her ears, and told her the most abominable falsehoods about the good and innocent Sir Verdour; when just as Sir Frankerico was about to forcibly carry away the Fair Margaret —

Why, just then, circumstances over which Mr. Verdant Green had no control, prevented the *denouement*, and the completion of 'the Legend.'

6

Mr. Verdant Green Joins a Northumberland Pic-Nic

Some weeks had passed away very pleasantly to all — pleasantly even to Mr. Verdant Green; for, although he had not renewed his apple-tree conversation with Miss Patty, and was making progress with his 'Legend of the Fair Margaret,' yet — it may possibly have been that the exertion to make 'dove' rhyme with 'love,' and 'gloom' with 'doom,' occupied his mind to the exclusion of needless sorrow — he contrived to make himself mournfully amiable, even if not tolerably happy, in the society of the fair enchantress.

The Honeywood party were indeed a model household; and rode, and drove, and walked, and fished, and sketched, as a large family of brothers and sisters might do — perhaps with a little more piquancy than is generally found in the home-made dish.

They had had more than one little friendly pic-nic and excursion, and had seen Warkworth, and grown excessively sentimental in its hermitage; they had lionised Alnwick, and

70

gone over its noble castle, and sat in Hotspur's chair, and fallen into raptures at the Duchess's bijou of a dairy, and viewed the pillared *passant* lion, with his tail blowing straight out (owing, probably, to the breezy nature of his position), and seen the Duke's herd of buffaloes tearing along their park with streaming manes; and they had gone back to Honeywood Hall, and received Honeywood guests, and been entertained by them in return.

But the squire was now about to give a pic-nic on a large scale; and as it was important, not only in its dimensions and preparations, but also in bringing about an occurrence that in no small degree affected Mr. Verdant Green's future life, it becomes his historian's duty to chronicle the event with the fulness that it merits. The pic-nic, moreover, deserves mention because it possessed an individuality of character, and was unlike the ordinary solemnities attending the pic-nics of every-day life.

In the first place, the party had to reach the appointed spot — which was Chillingham — in an unusual manner. At least half of the road that had to be traversed was impassable for carriages. Bridgeless brooks had to be crossed; and what were called 'roads' were little better than the beds of mountain torrents, and in wet weather might have been taken for such. Deep channels were worn in them by the rush of impetuous streams, and no known carriage-springs could have lived out such ruts. Carriages, therefore, in this part of the country, were out of the question. The squire did what was usual on such occasions: he appointed, as a rendezvous, a certain little inn at the extremity of the carriageable part of the road, and there all the party met, and left their chariots and horses. They then — after a little preparatory pic-nic, for many of them had come from long distances — took possession of certain wagons that were in waiting for them.

These wagons, though apparently of light build, were constructed for the country, and were capable of sustaining the severe test of the rough roads. Within them were lashed hay-sacks, which, when covered with railway rugs, formed sufficiently comfortable seats, on which the divisions of the party sat vis-a-vis, like omnibus travellers. Frank Delaval and a few others, on horses and ponies, as outriders, accompanied the wagon procession, which was by no means deficient in materials for the picturesque. The teams of horses were turned out to their best advantage, and decorated with flowers. The fore horse of each team bore his collar of little brass bells, which clashed out a wild music as they moved along. The ruddy-faced wagoners were in their shirt-sleeves, which were tied round with ribbons; they had gay ribbons also on their hats and whips, and did not lack bouquets and flowers for the further adornment of their persons. Altogether they were most theatrical-looking fellows, and appeared perfectly prepared to take their places in the *Sonnambula*, or any other opera in which decorated rustics have to appear and unanimously shout their joy and grief at the nightly rate of two shillings per head. The light summer dresses of the ladies helped to make an agreeable variety of colour, as the wagons moved slowly along the dark heathery hills, now by the side of a brawling brook, and now by a rugged road.

The joltings of these same roads were, as little Mr. Bouncer feelingly remarked, facts that must be felt to be believed. For, when the wheel of any vehicle is suddenly plunged into a rut or hole of a foot's depth, and from thence violently extracted with a jerk, plunge, and wrench, to be again dropped into another hole or rut, and withdrawn from thence in a like manner, — and when this process is being simultaneously repeated, with discordant variations, by other three wheels attached to the self-same vehicle, it will follow, as a matter of course, that the result of this experiment will be the violent agitation and commingling of the movable contents of the said vehicle; and, when these contents chance to take the semblance of humanity, it may readily be imagined what must have been the scene presented to the view as the pic-nic wagons, with their human freight, laboured thro' the mountain roads that led towards Chillingham.

But all this only gave a zest to the day's enjoyment; and, if Miss Patty Honeywood was unable to maintain her seat without assistance from her neighbour, Mr. Verdant Green, it is not at all improbable but that she approved of his kind attention, and that the other young ladies who were similarly situated accepted similar attentions with similar gratitude.

In this way they literally jogged along to Chillingham, where they alighted from their novel carriages and four, and then leisurely made their way to the castle. When they had sufficiently lionized it, and had strolled through the gardens, they went to have a look at the famous wild cattle. Our Warwickshire friends had frequently had a distant view of them; for the cattle kept together in a herd, and as their park was on the slope of a dark hill, they were visible from afar off as a moving white patch on the landscape. On the present occasion they found that the cattle, which numbered their full herd of about a hundred strong, were quietly grazing on the border of their pine-wood, where a few of their fellow-tenants, the original red deer, were lifting their enormous antlers. From their position the pic-nic party were unable to obtain a very near view of them; but the curiosity of the young ladies was strongly excited, and would not be allayed without a closer acquaintance with these formidable but beautiful creatures. And it therefore happened that, when the courageous Miss Bouncer proposed that they should make an incursion into the very territory of the Wild Cattle, her proposition was not only seconded, but was carried almost unanimously. It was in vain that Mr. Honeywood, and the seniors and chaperones of the party, reminded the younger people of the grisly head they had just seen hanging up in the lodge, and those straight sharp horns that had gored to death the brave keeper who had risked his own life to save his master's friend; it was in vain that Charles Larkyns, fearful for his Mary's sake, quoted the 'Bride of Lammermoor,' and urged the improbability of another Master of Ravenswood starting out of the bushes to the rescue of a second Lucy Ashton; it was in vain that anecdotes were told of the fury of these cattle — how they would single out some aged or wounded companion, and drive him out of the herd until he miserably died, and how they would hide themselves for days within their dark pine-wood, where no one dare attack them; it was in vain that Mr. Verdant Green reminded Miss Patty Honeywood of her narrow escape from Mr. Roarer, and warned her that her then danger was now increased a hundredfold; all in vain, for Miss Patty assured him that the cattle were as peaceable as they were beautiful, and that they only attacked people in self-defence when provoked or molested. So, as the young ladies were positively bent upon having a nearer view of the milk-white herd, the greater number of the gentlemen were obliged to accompany them.

It was no easy matter to get into the Wild Cattle's enclosure, as the boundary fence was of unusual height, and the difficulty of its being scaled by ladies was proportionately increased. Nevertheless, the fence and the difficulty were alike surmounted, and the party were safely landed within the park. They had promised to obey Mr. Honeywood's advice, and to abstain from that mill-stream murmur of conversation in which a party of young ladies usually indulge, and to walk quietly among the trees, across an angle of the park, at some two or three hundred yards' distance from the herd, so as not to unnecessarily attract their attention; and then to scale the fence at a point higher up the hill. Following this advice, they walked quietly across the mossy grass, keeping behind trees, and escaping the notice of the cattle. They had reached midway in their proposed path, and, with silent admiration, were watching the movements of the herd as they placidly grazed at a short distance from them, when Miss Bouncer, who was addicted to uncontrollable fits of laughter at improper seasons, was so tickled at some *sotto voce* remark of Frank Delaval's, that she burst into a hearty ringing laugh, which, ere she could smother its noise with her handkerchief, had startled the watchful ears of the monarch of the herd.

The Bull raised his magnificent head, and looked round in the direction from whence the disturbance had proceeded. As he perceived it, he sniffed the air, made a rapid movement with his pink-edged ears, and gave an ominous bellow. This signal awoke the attention of the other bulls, their wives, and children, who simultaneously left off grazing and commenced gazing. The bovine monarch gave another bellow, stamped upon the ground, lashed his tail, advanced about twenty yards in a threatening manner, and then paused, and gazed fixedly upon the pic-nic party and Miss Bouncer, who too late regretted her *malapropos* laugh.

'For heaven's sake!' whispered Mr. Honey-wood, 'do not speak; but get to the fence as quietly and quickly as you can.'

The young ladies obeyed, and forbore either to scream or faint — for the present. The Bull gave another stamp and bellow, and made a second advance. This time he came about fifty yards before he paused, and he was followed at a short distance, and at a walking pace, by the rest of the herd. The ladies retreated quietly, the gentlemen came after them, but the park-fence appeared to be at a terribly long distance, and it was evident that if the herd made a sudden rush upon them, nothing could save them — unless they could climb the trees; but this did not seem very practicable. Mr. Verdant Green, however, caught at the probability of such need, and anxiously looked round for the most likely tree for his purpose.

The Bull had made another advance, and was gaining upon them. It seemed curious that he should stand forth as the champion of the herd, and do all the roaring and stamping, while the other bulls remained mute, and followed with the rest of the herd, yet so it was; but there seemed no reason to disbelieve the unpleasant fact that the monarch's example would be imitated by his subjects. The herd had now drawn so near, and the young ladies had made such a comparatively slow retreat, that they were yet many yards' distant from the boundary fence, and it was quite plain that they could not reach it before the advancing milk-white mass would be hurled against them. Some of the young ladies were beginning to feel faint and hysterical, and their alarm was more or less shared by all the party.

It was now, by Charles Larkyns's advice, that the more active gentlemen mounted on to the lower branches of the wide-spreading trees, and, aided by others upon the ground, began to lift up the ladies to places of security. But, the party being a large one, this caring for its more valued but less athletic members was a business that could not be transacted without the expenditure of some little time and trouble, more, as it seemed, than could now be bestowed; for, the onward movement of the Chillingham Cattle was more rapid than the corresponding upward movement of the Northumbrian pic-nickers. And, even if Charles Larkyns's plan should have a favourable issue, it did not seem a very agreeable prospect to be detained up in a tree, with a century of bulls bellowing beneath, until casual assistance should arrive; and yet, what was this state of affairs when compared with the terrors of that impending fate from which, for some of them at least, there seemed no escape? Mr. Verdant Green fully realized the horrors of this alternative when he looked at Miss Patty Honeywood, who had not yet joined those ladies who, clinging fearfully to the boughs, and crouching among the branches like roosting guinea-fowls, were for the present in comparative safety, and out of the reach of the Cattle.

The monarch of the herd had now come within forty yards' distance, and then stopped, lashing his tail and bellowing defiance, as he appeared to be preparing for a final rush. Behind him, in a dense phalanx, white and terrible, were the rest of the herd. Suddenly, and before the Snowy Bull had made his advance, Frank Delaval, to the wondering fear of all, stepped boldly forth to meet him. As has been said, he was one of the equestrians of the party, and he carried a heavy-handled whip, furnished with a long and powerful lash. He wrapped this lash round his hand, and walked resolutely towards the Bull, fixing his eyes steadily upon him. The Bull chafed angrily, and stamped upon the ground, but did not advance. The herd, also, were motionless; but their dark, lustrous eyes were centred upon Frank Delaval's advancing figure. The members of the pic-nic party were also watching him with intense interest. If they could, they would have prevented his purpose; for to all appearance he was about to lose his own life in order that the rest of the party might gain time to reach a place of safety. The very expectation of this prevented many of the ladies availing themselves of the opportunity thus so boldly purchased, and they stood transfixed with terror and astonishment, breathlessly awaiting the result.

They watched him draw near the wild white Bull, who stood there yet, foaming and stamping up the turf, but not advancing. His huge horned head was held erect, and his mane bristled up, as he looked upon the adversary who thus dared to brave him. He suffered Frank Delaval to approach him, and only betrayed a consciousness of his presence by his heavy snorting, angry lashing of the tail, and quick motion of his bright eye. All this time the young man had looked the Bull steadfastly in the front, and had drawn near him with an equal and steady step. Suppressed screams broke from more than one witness of his bravery, when he at length stood within a step of his huge adversary. He gazed fixedly into the Bull's eyes, and, after a moment's pause, suddenly raised his riding-whip, and lashed the animal heavily over the shoulders. The Bull tossed round, and roared with fury. The whole herd became agitated, and other bulls trotted up to support their monarch.

Still looking him steadfastly in the eyes, Frank Delaval again raised his heavy whip, and lashed him more severely than before. The Wild Bull butted down, swerved round, and dashed out with his heels. As he did so, Frank again struck him heavily with the whip, and, at the same time, blew a piercing signal on the boatswain's whistle that he usually carried with him. The sudden shriek of the whistle appeared to put the *coup de grâce* to the young man's bold attack, for the animal had no sooner heard it than he tossed up his head and threw forward his ears, as though to ask from whence the novel noise proceeded. Frank Delaval again blew a piercing shriek on the whistle; and when the Wild Bull heard it, and once more felt the stinging lash of the heavy whip, he swerved round, and with a bellow of pain and fury trotted back to the herd. The young man blew another shrill whistle, and cracked the long lash of his whip until its echoes reverberated like so many pistol-shots. The Wild Bull's trot increased to a gallop, and he and the whole herd of the Chillingham Cattle dashed rapidly away from the pic-nic party, and in a little time were lost to view in the recesses of their forest.

'Thank God!' said Mr. Honeywood; and it was echoed in the hearts of all. But the Squire's emotion was too deep for words, as he went to meet Frank Delaval, and pressed him by the hand.

'Get the women outside the park as quickly as possible,' said Frank, 'and I will join you.'

But when this was done, and Mr. Honeywood had returned to him, he found him lying motionless beneath the tree.

7

Mr. Verdant Green has an Inkling of the Future

Among other things that Mr. Honeywood had thoughtfully provided for the pic-nic was a flask of pale brandy, which, for its better preservation, he had kept in his own pocket. This was fortunate, as it enabled the Squire to make use of it for Frank Delaval's recovery. He had fainted: his concentrated courage and resolution had borne him bravely up to a certain point, and then his overtaxed energies had given way when the necessity for their exertion was removed. When he had come to himself, he appeared to be particularly thankful that there had not been a spectator of (what he deemed to be) his unpardonable foolishness in giving way to a weakness that he considered should be indulged in by none other than faint-hearted women; and he earnestly begged the Squire to be silent on this little episode in the day's adventure.

When they had left the Wild Cattle's park, and had joined the rest of the party, Frank Delaval received the hearty thanks that he so richly deserved; and this, with such an exuberant display of feminine gratitude as to lead Mr. Bouncer to observe that, if Mr. Delaval chose to take a mean advantage of his position, he could have immediately proposed to two-thirds of the ladies, without the possibility of their declining his offer: at which remark Mr. Verdant Green experienced an uncomfortable sensation, as he thought of the probable issue of events if Mr. Delaval should partly act upon Mr. Bouncer's suggestion, by selecting one young lady — his cousin Patty — and proposing to her. This reflection became strengthened into a determination to set the matter at rest, decide his doubts, and put an end to his suspense, by taking the first opportunity to renew with Miss Patty that most interesting apple-tree conversation that had been interrupted by Mr. Bouncer at such a critical moment.

The pic-nic party, broken up into couples and groups, slowly made their way up the hill to Ros Castle — the doubly-intrenched British fort on the summit — where the dinner was to take place. It was a rugged road, running along the side of the park, bounded by rocky banks, and shaded by trees. It was tenanted as usual by a Faw gang, — a band of gipsies, whose wild and gay attire, with their accompaniments of tents, carts, horses, dogs, and fires, added picturesqueness to the scene. With the characteristic of their race — which appears to be a shrewd mixture of mendicity and mendacity — they at once abandoned their business of tinkering and peg-making; and, resuming their other business of fortune-telling and begging, they judiciously distributed themselves among the various divisions of the pic-nic party.

Mr. Verdant Green was strolling up the hill lost in meditation, and so inattentive to the wiles of Miss Eleonora Morkin, and her sister Letitia Jane (two fascinating young ladies who were bent upon turning the pic-nic to account), that they had left him, and had forcibly attached themselves to Mr. Poletiss (a soft young gentleman from the neighbour-hood of Wooler), when a gipsy woman, with a baby at her back and two children at her heels, singled out our hero as a not unlikely victim, and began at once to tell his fate, dispensing with the aid of stops:—

'May the heavens rain blessings on your head my pretty gentleman give the poor gipsy a piece of silver to buy her a bit for the bairns and I can read by the lines in your face my pretty gentleman that you're born to ride in a golden coach and wear buckles of diemints and that your heart's opening like a flower to help the poor gipsy to get her a trifle for her poor famishing bairns that I see the tears of pity astanding like pearls in your eyes my pretty gentleman and may you never know the want of the shilling that I see you're going to give the poor gipsy who will send you all the rich blessings of heaven if you will but cross her hand with the bright pieces of silver that are not half so bright as the sweet eyes of the lady that's awaiting and athinking of you my pretty gentleman.'

This unpunctuated exhortation of the dark-eyed prophetess was here diverted into a new channel by the arrival of Miss Patty Honeywood, who had left her cousin Frank, and had brought her sketch-book to the spot where 'the pretty gentleman' and the fortune-teller were standing.

'I do so want to draw a real gipsy,' she said. 'I have never yet sketched one; and this is a good opportunity. These little brownies of children, with their Italian faces and hair, are very picturesque in their rags.'

'Oh! do draw them!' said Verdant enthusiastically, as he perceived that the rest of the party had passed out of sight. 'It is a capital opportunity, and I dare say they will have no objection to be sketched.'

'May the heavens be the hardest bed you'll ever have to lie on my pretty rosebud,' said the unpunctuating descendant of John Faa, as she addressed herself to Miss Patty; 'and you're welcome to take the poor gipsy's pictur and to cross her hand with the shining silver while she reads the stars and picks you out a prince of a husband and twelve pretty bairns like the — '

'No, no!' said Miss Patty, checking the gipsy in her bounteous promises. 'I'll give you something for letting me sketch you, but I won't have my fortune told. I know it already; at least as much as I care to know.' A speech which Mr. Verdant Green interpreted thus: Frank Delaval has proposed, and has been accepted.

'Pray don't let me keep you from the rest of the party,' said Miss Patty to our hero, while the gipsy shot out fragments of persuasive oratory. 'I can get on very well by myself.'

'She wants to get rid of me,' thought Verdant. 'I dare say her cousin is coming back to her.' But he said, 'At any rate let me stay until Mr. Delaval rejoins you.'

'Oh! he is gone on with the rest, like a polite man. The Miss Maxwells and their cousins were all by themselves.'

'But *you* are all by *yourself*, and, by your own showing, I ought to prove my politeness by staying with you.'

'I suppose that is Oxford logic,' said Miss Patty, as she went on with her sketch of the two gipsy children. 'I wish these small persons would stand quiet. Put your hands on your stick, my boy, and not before your face. — But there are the Miss Morkins, with one gentleman for the two; and I dare say you would much rather be with Miss Eleonora. Now, wouldn't you?' and the young lady, as she rapidly sketched the figures before her, stole a sly look at the enamoured gentleman by her side, who forthwith protested, in an excited and confused manner, that he would rather stand near her for one minute than walk and talk for a whole day with the Miss Morkins; and then, having made this (for him) unusually strong avowal, he timidly blushed, and retired within himself.

'Oh yes! I dare say,' said Miss Patty; 'but I don't believe in compliments. If you choose to victimize yourself by staying here, of course you can do so. — Look at me, little girl; you needn't be frightened; I shan't eat you. — And perhaps you can be useful. I want some water to wash-in these figures; and if they were literally washed in it, it would be very much to their advantage, wouldn't it?'

Of course it would; and of course Mr. Verdant Green was delighted to obey the command. 'What spirits she is in!' he thought, as he dipped the little can of water into the spring. 'I dare say it is because she and her

cousin Frank have come to an understanding.'

'If you are anxious to hear a fortune told,'
said Miss Patty, 'here is the old gipsy coming
back to us, and you had better let her tell
yours.'

'I am afraid that I know it.'

'And do you like the prospect of it?'

'Not at all!' and as he said this Mr. Verdant
Green's countenance fell. Singularly enough,
a shade of sadness also stole over Miss Patty's
sunny face. What could he mean?

A somewhat disagreeable silence was
broken by the gipsy most volubly echoing
Miss Patty's request.

'You had better let her tell you your
fortune,' said the young lady; 'perhaps it may
be an improvement on what you expected.
And I shall be able to make a better sketch of
her in her true character of a fortune-teller.'

Then, like as Martivalle inspected Quentin
Durward's palm, according to the form of
the mystic arts which he practised, so the
swarthy prophetess opened her Book of Fate,
and favoured Mr. Verdant Green with choice
extracts from its contents. First, she told the
pretty gentleman a long rigmarole about
the stars, and a planet that ought to have
shone upon him, but didn't. Then she
discoursed of a beautiful young lady, with a

heart as full of love as a pomegranate was full of seeds, — painting, in pretty exact colours, a lively portraiture of Miss Patty, which was no very difficult task, while the fair original was close at hand; nevertheless, the infatuated pretty gentleman was deeply impressed with the gipsy narrative, and began to think that the practice and knowledge of the occult sciences may, after all, have been handed down to the modern representatives of the ancient Egyptians. He was still further impressed with this belief when the gipsy proceeded to tell him that he was passionately attached to the pomegranate-hearted young lady, but that his path of true love was crossed by a rival — a dark man.

Frank Delaval! This is really most extraordinary! thought Mr. Verdant Green, who was not familiar with a fortune-teller's stock in trade; and he waited with some anxiety for the further unravelling of his fate.

The cunning gipsy saw this, and broadly hinted that another piece of silver placed upon the junction of two cross lines in the pretty gentleman's right palm would materially propitiate the stars, and assist in the happy solution of his fortune. When the hint had been taken she pursued her romantic narrative. Her elaborate but discursive summing-up comprehended the triumph of Mr. Verdant Green, the defeat of the dark man, the marriage of the former to the pomegranate-hearted young lady, a yellow carriage and four white horses with long tails, and, last but certainly not least, a family of twelve children: at which childish termination Miss Patty laughed, and asked our hero if that was the fate that he had dreaded?

Her sketch being concluded, she remunerated her models so munificently as to draw down upon her head a rapid series of the most wordy and incoherent blessings she had ever heard, under cover of which she effected her escape, and proceeded with her companion to rejoin the others. They were not very far in advance. The gipsies had beset them at divers points in their progress, and had made no small number of them yield to their importunities to cross their hands with silver. When the various members of the pic-nic party afterwards came to compare notes as to the fortunes that had been told them, it was discovered that a remarkable similarity pervaded the fates of all, though their destinies were greatly influenced by the amount expended in crossing the hand; and it was observable that the number of children promised to bless the nuptial tie was also regulated by a sliding scale of payment — the largest payers being rewarded with the assurance of the largest families. It was also discovered that the description of the favoured lover was invariably the verbal delineation of the lady or gentleman who chanced to be at that time walking with the person whose fortune was being told — a prophetic discrimination worthy of all praise, since it had the pretty good security of being correct in more than one case, and in the other cases there was the chance of the prophecy coming true, however improbable present events would appear. Thus, Miss Eleonora Morkin received, and was perfectly satisfied with, a description of Mr. Poletiss; while Miss Letitia Jane Morkin was made supremely happy with a promise of a similarly-described gentleman; until the two sisters had compared notes, when they discovered that the same husband had been promised to both of them — which by no means improved their sororal amiability.

As Verdant walked up the hill with Miss Patty, he thought very seriously on his feelings towards her, and pondered what might be the nature of her feelings in regard to him. He believed that she was engaged to her cousin Frank. All her little looks, and acts, and words to himself, he could construe as the mere tokens of the friendship of a warm-hearted girl. If she was inclined to a little flirtation, there was then an additional reason for her notice of him. Then he thought that she was of far too noble a disposition to lead him on to a love which she could not, or might not wish to, return; and that she would not have said and done many little things that he fondly recalled, unless she had chosen to show him that he was dearer to her than a mere friend. Having ascended to the heights of happiness by this thought, Verdant immediately plunged from thence into the depths of misery, by calling to mind various other little things that she had said and done in connection with her cousin; and he again forced himself into the conviction that in Frank Delaval he had a rival, and, what was more, a successful one. He determined, before the day was over, to end his tortures of suspense by putting to Miss Patty the plain question whether or no she was engaged to her cousin, and to trust to her kindness to forgive the question if it was an impertinent one. He was unable to do this for the present, partly from lack of courage, and partly from the too close neighbourhood of others of the party; but he concocted several sentences that seemed to him to be admirably adapted to bring about the desired result.

'How abstracted you are!' said Miss Patty to him rather abruptly. 'Why don't you make yourself agreeable? For the last three minutes you have not taken your eyes off Kitty.' (She was walking just before them, with her cousin Frank.) 'What were you thinking about?'

Perhaps it was that he was suddenly roused from deep thought, and had no time to frame an evasive reply; but at any rate Mr. Verdant Green answered, 'I was thinking that Mr. Delaval had proposed, and had been accepted.' And then he was frightened at what he had said; for Miss Patty looked confused and surprised. 'I see that it is so,' he sighed, and his heart sank within him.

'How did you find it out?' she replied. 'It is a secret for the present; and we do not wish any one to know of it.'

'My dear Patty,' said Frank Delaval, who had waited for them to come up, 'wherever have you been? We thought the gipsies had stolen you. I am dying to tell you my fortune. I was with Miss Maxwell at the time, and the old woman described her to me as my future wife. The fortune-teller was slightly on the wrong tack, wasn't she?' So Frank Delaval and the Misses Honeywood laughed; and Mr. Verdant Green also laughed in a very savage manner; and they all seemed to think it a very capital joke, and walked on together in very capital spirits.

'My last hope is gone!' thought Verdant. 'I have now heard my fate from her own lips.'

8

Mr. Verdant Green Crosses
the Rubicon

The pic-nic dinner was laid near to the brow of the hill of Ros Castle, on the shady side of the park wall. In this cool retreat, with the thick summer foliage to screen them from the hot sun, they could feast undisturbed either by the Wild Cattle or the noonday glare, and drink in draughts of beauty from the wide-spread landscape before them.

The hill on which they were seated was broken up into the most picturesque undulations; here, the rock cropped out from the mossy turf; there, the blaeberries (the bilberries of more southern counties) clustered in myrtle-like bushes. The intrenched hill sloped down to a rich plain, spreading out for many miles, traversed by the great north road, and dotted over with hamlets. Then came a brown belt of sand, and a broken white line of breakers; and then the sea, flecked with crested waves, and sails that glimmered in the dreamy distance. Holy Island was also in sight, together with the rugged Castle of Bamborough, and the picturesque groups of the Staple and the Farn Islands, covered with sea-birds, and circled with pearls of foam.

The immediate foreground presented a very cheering prospect to hungry folks. The snowy table-cloth — held down upon the grass by fragments of rock against the surprise of high winds — was dappled over with loins of lamb, and lobster salads, and pigeon-pies, and veal cakes, and grouse, and game, and ducks, and cold fowls, and ruddy hams, and helpless tongues, and cool cucumbers, and pickled salmon, and roast-beef of old England, and oyster patties, and venison pasties, and all sorts of pastries, and jellies, and custards, and ice: to say nothing of piles of peaches, and nectarines, and grapes, and melons, and pines. Everything had been remembered — even the salt, and the knives and forks, which are usually forgotten at *alfresco* entertainments. All this was very cheering, and suggestive of enjoyment and creature comforts. Wines and humbler liquids stood around; and, for the especial delectation of the ladies, a goodly supply of champagne lay cooling itself in some ice-pails, under the tilt of the cart that had brought it. This cart-tilt, draped over with loose sacking, formed a very good imitation of a gipsy tent, that did not in the least detract from the rusticity of the scene, more especially as close behind it was burning a gipsy fire, surmounted by a triple gibbet, on which hung a kettle, melodious even then, and singing through its swan-like neck an intimation of its readiness to aid, at a moment's notice, in the manufacture of whisky-toddy.

The dinner was a very merry affair. The gentlemen vied with the servants in attending to the wants of the ladies, and were assiduous in the duties of cutting and carving; while the sharp popping of the champagne, and the heavier artillery of the pale ale and porter bottles, made a pleasant fusillade. Little Mr. Bouncer was especially deserving of notice. He sat with his legs in the shape of the letter V inverted, his legs being forced to retain their position from the fact of three dishes of various dimensions being arranged between them in a diminuendo passage. These three dishes he vigorously attacked, not only on his own account, but also on behalf of his neighbours, more especially Miss Fanny Green, who reclined by his side in an oriental posture, and made a table of her lap. The disposition of the rest of the *dramatis personae* was also noticeable, as also their positions — their sitting *a la* Turk or tailor, and their *degages* attitudes and costumes. Charles Larkyns had got by Mary Green; Mr. Poletiss was placed, sandwich-like, between the two Miss Morkins, who were both making love to him at once; Frank Delaval was sitting in a similar fashion between the two Miss Honeywoods, who were not, however, both making love to him at once; and on the other side of Miss Patty was Mr. Verdant Green. The infatuated young man could not drag himself away from his conqueror. Although, from her own confession, he had learnt what he had many times suspected — that Frank Delaval had proposed and had been accepted — yet he still felt a pleasure in burning his wings and fluttering round his light of love. 'An affection of the heart cannot be cured at a moment's notice,' thought Verdant; 'to-morrow I will endeavour to begin the task of forgetting — to-day, remembrance is too recent; besides, every one is expected to enjoy himself at a pic-nic, and I must appear to do the same.'

But it did not seem as though Miss Patty had any intention of allowing those in her immediate vicinity to betake themselves to the dismals, or to the produce of wet-blankets, for she was in the very highest spirits, and insisted, as it were, that those around her should catch the contagion of her cheerfulness. And it accordingly happened that Mr. Verdant Green seemed to be as merry as was old King Cole, and laughed and talked as though black care was anywhere else than between himself and Miss Patty Honeywood.

Close behind Miss Patty was the gipsy-tent-looking cart-tilt; and when the dinner was over, and there was a slight change of places, while the fragments were being cleared away and the dessert and wine were being placed on the table — that is to say, the cloth — Miss Patty, under pretence of escaping from a ray of sunshine that had pierced the trees and found its way to her face, retreated a yard or so, and crouched beneath the pseudo gipsy-tent. And what so natural but that Mr. Verdant Green should also find the sun disagreeable, and should follow his light of love, to burn his wings a little more, and flutter round her fascinations? At any rate, whether natural or no, Verdant also drew back a yard or so, and found himself half within the cart-tilt, and very close to Miss Patty.

The pic-nic party were stretched at their ease upon the grass, drinking wine, munching fruit, talking, laughing, and flirting, with the blue sea before them and the bluer sky above them, when said the squire in heroic strain,

'Song alone is wanting to crown our feast! Charles Larkyns, you have not only the face of a singer, but, as we all know, you have the voice of one. I therefore call upon you to set our minstrels an example; and, as a propitiatory measure, I beg to propose your health, with eulogistic thanks for the song you are about to sing!' Which was unanimously seconded amid laughter and cheers; and the pop of the champagne bottles gave Charles Larkyns the key-note for his song. It was suited to the occasion (perhaps it was composed for it?), being a paean for a pic-nic, and it stated (in chorus) —

'Then these aids to success
Should a pic-nic possess
For the cup of its joy to be brimming:
Three things there should shine
Fair, agreeable, and fine —
The Weather, the Wine, and the Women!'

A rule of pic-nics which, if properly worked out, could not fail to answer.

Other songs followed; and Mr. Poletiss, being a young gentleman of a meek appearance and still meeker voice, lyrically informed the company that 'Oh! he was a pirate bold, The scourge of the wide, wide sea, With a murd'rous thirst for gold, And a life that was wild and free!' And when Mr. Poletiss arrived at this point, he repeated the last word two or three times over — just as if he had been King George the Third visiting Whitbread's Brewery —

'Grains, grains!' said majesty, 'to fill their crops?
Grains, grains! that comes from hops — yes, hops, hops, hops!'

So Mr. Poletiss sang, 'And a life that was wild and free, free, free, And a life that was wild and free.' To this charming lyric there was a chorus of, 'Then hurrah for the pirate bold, And hurrah for the rover wild, And hurrah for the yellow gold, And hurrah for the ocean's child!' the mild enunciation of which highly moral and appropriate chant appeared to give Mr. Poletiss great satisfaction, as he turned his half-shut eyes to the sky, and fashioned his mouth into a smile. Mr. Bouncer's love for a chorus was conspicuously displayed on this occasion; and Miss Eleonora and Miss Letitia Jane Morkin added their feeble trebles to the hurrahs with which Mr. Poletiss, in his George the Third fashion, meekly hailed the advantages to be derived from a pirate's career.

But what was Mr. Verdant Green doing all

this time? The sunbeam had pursued him, and proved so annoying that he had found it necessary to withdraw altogether into the shade of the pseudo gipsy-tent. Miss Patty Honeywood had made such room for him that she was entirely hidden from the rest of the party by the rude drapery of the tent. By the time that Mr. Poletiss had commenced his piratical song, Miss Patty and Verdant were deep in a whispered conversation. It was she who had started the conversation, and it was about the gipsy and her fortune-telling.

Just when Mr. Poletiss had given his first imitation of King George, and was mildly plunging into his hurrah chorus, Mr. Verdant Green — whose timidity, fears, and depression of spirits had somewhat been dispelled and alleviated by the allied powers of Miss Patty and the champagne — was speaking thus: 'And do you really think that she was only inventing, and that the dark man she spoke of was a creature of her own imagination?'

'Of course!' answered Miss Patty; 'you surely don't believe that she could have meant any one in particular, either in the gentleman's case or in the lady's?'

'But, in the lady's, she evidently described *you*.'

'Very likely! just as she would have

described any other young lady who might have chanced to be with you: Miss Morkin, for example. The gipsy knew her trade.'

'Many true words are spoken in jest. Perhaps it was not altogether idly that she spoke; perhaps I *did* care for the lady she described.'

The sunbeam must surely have penetrated through the tent's coarse covering, for both Miss Patty and Mr. Verdant Green were becoming very hot — hotter even than they had been under the apple-tree in the orchard. Mr. Poletiss was all this time giving his imitations of George the Third, and lyrically expressing his opinion as to the advantages to be derived from the profession of a pirate; and, as his song was almost as long as 'Chevy Chase,' and mainly consisted of a chorus, which was energetically led by Mr. Bouncer, there was noise enough made to drown any whispered conversation in the pseudo gipsy-tent.

'But,' continued Verdant, 'perhaps the lady she described did not care for me, or she would not have given all her love to the dark man.'

'I think,' faltered Miss Patty, 'the gipsy seemed to say that the lady preferred the light man. But you do not believe what she told you?'

'I would have done so a few days ago — if it had been repeated by you.'

'I scarcely know what you mean.'

'Until to-day I had hoped. It seems that I have built my hopes on a false foundation, and one word of yours has crumbled them into the dust!'

This pretty sentence embodied an idea that he had stolen from his own *Legend of the Fair Margaret*. He felt so much pride in his property that, as Miss Patty looked slightly bewildered and remained speechless, he reiterated the little quotation about his crumbling hopes.

'Whatever can I have done,' said the young lady, with a smile, 'to cause such a ruin?'

'It caused you no pain to utter the words,' replied Verdant; 'and why should it? but, to me, they tolled the knell of my happiness.' (This was another quotation from his *Legend*.)

'Then hurrah for the pirate bold. And hurrah for the rover wild!' sang the meek Mr. Poletiss.

Miss Patty Honeywood began to suspect that Mr. Verdant Green had taken too much champagne!

'What *do* you mean?' she said. 'Whatever have I said or done to you that you make use of such remarkable expressions?'

'And hurrah for the yellow gold, And hurrah for the ocean's child!' chorussed Messrs. Poletiss, Bouncer, and Co.

Looking as sentimental as his spectacles would allow, Mr. Verdant Green replied in verse —

"'Hopes that once we've loved to cherish
May fade and droop, but never perish!'

as Shakespeare says.' (Although he modestly attributed this sentiment to the Swan of Avon, it was, nevertheless, another quotation from his own *Legend*.) 'And it is my case. *I* cannot forget the Past, though *you* may!'

'Really you are as enigmatical as the Sphinx!' said Miss Patty, who again thought of Mr. Verdant Green in connection with champagne. 'Pray condescend to speak more plainly, for I was never clever at finding out riddles.'

'And have you forgotten what you said to me, in reply to a question that I asked you, as we came up the hill?'

'Yes, I have quite forgotten. I dare say I said many foolish things; but what was the particular foolish thing that so dwells on your mind?'

'If it is so soon forgotten, it is not worth repeating.'

106

'Oh, it is! Pray gratify my curiosity. I am sorry my bad memory should have given you any pain.'

'It was not your bad memory, but your words.'

'My bad words?'

'No, not bad; but words that shut out a bright future, and changed my life to gloom.' (The *Legend* again.)

Miss Patty looked more perplexed than ever; while Mr. Poletiss politely filled up the gap of silence with an imitation of King George the Third.

'I really do not know what you mean,' said Miss Patty. 'If I have said or done anything that has caused you pain, I can assure you it was quite unwittingly on my part, and I am very sorry for it; but, if you will tell me what it was, perhaps I may be able to explain it away, and disabuse your mind of a false impression.'

'I am quite sure that you did not intend to pain me,' replied Verdant; 'and I know that it was presumptuous in me to think as I did. It was scarcely probable that you would feel as I felt; and I ought to have made up my mind to it, and have borne my sufferings with a patient heart.' (The *Legend* again!) 'And yet when the shock *does* come, it is very hard to be borne.'

Miss Patty's bright eyes were dilated with wonder, and she again thought of Mr. Verdant Green in connection with champagne. Mr. Poletiss was still taking his pirate through all sorts of flats and sharps, and chromatic imitations of King George.

'But, what *is* this shock?' asked Miss Patty. 'Perhaps I can relieve it; and I ought to do so if it came through my means.'

'You cannot help me,' said Verdant. 'My suspicions were confirmed by your words, and they have sealed my fate.'

'But you have not yet told me what those words were, and I must really insist upon knowing,' said Miss Patty, who had begun to look very seriously perplexed.

'And, can you have forgotten!' was the reply. 'Do you not remember, that, as we came up the hill, I put a certain question to you about Mr. Delaval having proposed and having been accepted?'

'Yes! I remember it very well! And, what then?'

'And, what then!' echoed Mr. Verdant Green, in the greatest wonder at the young lady's calmness; 'what then! why, when you told me that he *had* been accepted, was not that sufficient for me to know? — to know that all my love had been given to one who was another's, and that all my hopes were blighted! was

108

not this sufficient to crush me, and to change the colour of my life?' And Verdant's face showed that, though he might be quoting from his *Legend*, he was yet speaking from his heart.

'Oh! I little expected this!' faltered Miss Patty, in real grief; 'I little thought of this. Why did you not speak sooner to some one — to me, for instance — and have spared yourself this misery? If you had been earlier made acquainted with Frank's attachment, you might then have checked your own. I did not ever dream of this!' And Miss Patty, who had turned pale, and trembled with agitation, could not restrain a tear.

'It is very kind of you thus to feel for me!' said Verdant; 'and all I ask is, that you will still remain my friend.'

'Indeed, I will. And I am sure Kitty will always wish to be the same. She will be sadly grieved to hear of this; for, I can assure you that she had no suspicion you were attached to her.'

'Attached to HER!' cried Verdant, with vast surprise. 'What ever do you mean?'

'Have you not been telling me of your secret love for her?' answered Miss Patty, who again turned her thoughts to the champagne.

'Love for *her*? No! nothing of the kind.'

'What! and not spoken about your grief

when I told you that Frank Delaval had proposed to her, and had been accepted?'

'Proposed to *her*?' cried Verdant, in a kind of dreamy swoon.

'Yes! to whom else do you suppose he would propose?'

'To *you*!'

'To ME!'

'Yes, to you! Why, have you not been telling me that you were engaged to him?'

'Telling you that *I* was engaged to Frank!' rejoined Miss Patty. 'Why, what could put such an idea into your head? Frank is engaged to Kitty. You asked me if it was not so; and I told you, yes, but that it was a secret at present. Why, then of whom were *you* talking?'

'Of *you*!'

'Of *me*?'

'Yes, of you!' And the scales fell from the eyes of both, and they saw their mutual mistake.

There was a silence, which Verdant was the first to break.

'It seems that love is really blind. I now perceive how we have been playing at cross questions and crooked answers. When I asked you about Mr. Delaval, my thoughts were wholly of you, and I spoke of you, and not of your sister, as you imagined; and I fancied

110

that you answered not for your sister, but for yourself. When I spoke of my attachment, it did not refer to your sister, but to you.'

'To me?' softly said Miss Patty, as a delicious tremor stole over her.

'To you, and to you alone,' answered Verdant. The great stumbling-block of his doubts was now removed, and his way lay clear before him. Then, after a momentary pause to nerve his determination, and without further prelude, or beating about the bush, he said, 'Patty — my dear Miss Honeywood — I love you! do you love me?'

There it was at last! The dreaded question over which he had passed so many hours of thought, was at length spoken. The elaborate sentences that he had devised for its introduction, had all been forgotten; and his artificial flowers of oratory had been exchanged for those simpler blossoms of honesty and truth — 'I love you — do you love me?' He had imagined that he should put the question to her when they were alone in some quiet room; or, better still, when they were wandering together in some sequestered garden walk or shady lane; and, now, here he had unexpectedly, and undesignedly, found his opportunity at a pic-nic dinner, with half a hundred people close beside him, and his ears assaulted with a songster's praises of piracy and murder. Strange accompaniments to a declaration of the tender passion! But, like others before him, he had found that there was no such privacy as that of a crowd — the fear of interruption probably adding a spur to determination, while the laughter and busy talking of others assist to fill up awkward pauses of agitation in the converse of the loving couple.

Despite the heat, Miss Patty's cheeks paled for a moment, as Verdant put to her that question, 'Do you love me?' Then a deep blush stole over them, as she whispered 'I do.'

What need for more? what need for pressure of hands or lips, and vows of love and constancy? What need even for the elder and more desperate of the Miss Morkins to maliciously suggest that Mr. Poletiss — who had concluded, amid a great display of approbation (probably because it *was* concluded) his mild piratical chant, and his imitations of King George the Third — should call upon Mr. Verdant Green, who, as she understood, was a very good singer? 'And, dear me! where could he have gone to, when he was here just now, you know! and, good gracious! why there he was, under the cart-tilt — and well, I never was so surprised — Miss Martha Honeywood with him, flirting now, I dare say? shouldn't you think so?'

No need for this stroke of generalship! No

need for Miss Letitia Jane Morkin to prompt Miss Fanny Green to bring her brother out of his retirement. No need for Mr. Frank Delaval to say 'I thought you were never going to slip from your moorings!' Or for little Mr. Bouncer to cry, 'Yoicks! unearthed at last!' No need for anything, save the parental sanction to the newly-formed engagement. Mr. Verdant Green had proposed, and had been accepted; and Miss Patty Honeywood could exclaim with Schiller's heroine, 'Ich habe gelebt und geliebet! — I have lived, and have loved!'

9

Mr. Verdant Green Asks Papa

Miss Morkin met with her reward before many hours. The pic-nic party were on their way home, and had reached within a short distance of the inn where their wagons had to be exchanged for carriages. It has been mentioned that, among the difficulties of the way, they had to drive through bridgeless brooks; and one of these was not half-a-mile distant from the inn.

It happened that the mild Mr. Poletiss was seated at the tail end of the wagon, next to the fair Miss Morkin, who was laying violent siege to him, with a battery of words, if not of charms. If the position of Mr. Poletiss, as to deliverance from his fair foe, was a difficult one, his position, as to maintaining his seat during the violent throes and tossings to and fro of the wagon, was even more difficult; for Mr. Poletiss's mildness of voice was surpassed by his mildness of manner, and he was far too timid to grasp at the side of the wagon by placing his arm behind the fair Miss Morkin, lest it should be supposed that he was assuming the privileged position of a partner in a *valse*. Mr. Poletiss, therefore, whenever they jolted through ruts or brooks, held on to his hay hassock, and preserved his equilibrium as best he could.

On the same side of the wagon, but at its upper and safer end, was seated Mr. Bouncer, who was not slow to perceive that a very slight *accident* would destroy Mr. Poletiss's equilibrium; and the little gentleman's fertile brain speedily concocted a plan, which he forthwith communicated to Miss Fanny Green, who sat next to him. It was this:— that when they were plunging through the brook, and every one was swaying to and fro, and was thrown off their balance, Mr. Bouncer should take advantage of the critical moment, and (by accident, of course!) give Miss Fanny Green a heavy push; this would drive her against her next neighbour, Miss Patty Honeywood; who, from the recoil, would literally be precipitated into the arms of Mr. Verdant Green, who would be pushed against Miss Letitia Jane Morkin, who would be driven against her sister, who would be propelled against Mr. Poletiss, and thus give him that *coup de grâce*, which, as Mr. Bouncer hoped, would have the effect of quietly tumbling him out of the wagon, and partially ducking him in the brook. 'It won't hurt him,' said the little gentleman; 'it'll do him good. The brook ain't deep, and a bath will be pleasant such a day as this. He can dry his clothes at the inn, and get some steaming toddy, if he's afraid of catching cold. And it will be such a lark to see him in the water. Perhaps Miss Morkin will take a header, and plunge in to save him; and he will promise her his hand, and a medal from the Humane Society! The wagon will be sure to give a heavy lurch as we come up out of the brook, and what so natural as that we should all be jolted, against each other?' It is not necessary to state whether or no Miss Fanny Green seconded or opposed Mr. Bouncer's motion; suffice it to say that it was carried out.

They had reached the brook. Miss Morkin was exclaiming, 'Oh, dear! here's another of those dreadful brooks — the last, I hope, for I always feel so timid at water, and I never bathe at the sea-side without shutting my eyes and being pushed into it by the old woman — and, my goodness! here we are, and I feel convinced that we shall all be thrown in by those dreadful wagoners, who are quite tipsy I'm sure — don't you think so, Mr. Poletiss?'

But, ere Mr. Poletiss could meekly respond, the horses had been quickened into a trot, the wagon had gone down into the brook — through it — and was bounding up the opposite side — everybody was holding

116

tightly to anything that came nearest to hand — when, at that fatal moment, little Mr. Bouncer gave the preconcerted push, which was passed on, unpremeditatedly, from one to another, until it had gained its electrical climax in the person of Miss Morkin, who, with a shriek, was propelled against Mr. Poletiss, and gave the necessary momentum that toppled him from the wagon into the brook. But, dreadful to relate, Mr. Bouncer's practical joke did not terminate at this fixed point. Mr. Poletiss, in the suddenness of his fall, naturally struck out at any straw that might save him; and the straw that he caught was the dress of Miss Morkin. She being at that moment off her balance, and the wagon moving rapidly at an angle of 45°, was unable to save herself from following the example of Mr. Poletiss, and she also toppled over into the brook. A third victim would have been added to Mr. Bouncer's list, had not Mr. Verdant Green, with considerable presence of mind, plucked Miss Letitia Jane Morkin from the violent hands that her sister was laying upon her, in making the same endeavours after safety that had been so futilely employed by the luckless Mr. Poletiss.

No sooner had he fallen with a splash into the brook, than Miss Eleonora Morkin was not only after but upon him. This was so far fortunate for the lady, that it released her with only a partial wetting, and she speedily rolled from off her submerged companion on to the shore; but it rendered the ducking of Mr. Poletiss a more complete one, and he scrambled from the brook, dripping and heavy with wet, like an old ewe emerging from a sheep-shearing tank. The wagon had been immediately stopped, and Mr. Bouncer and the other gentlemen had at once sprung down to Miss Morkin's assistance. Being thus surrounded by a male bodyguard, the young lady could do no less than go into hysterics, and fall into the nearest gentleman's arms, and as this gentleman was little Mr. Bouncer he was partially punished for his practical joke. Indeed, he afterwards declared that a severe cold which troubled him for the next fortnight was attributable to his having held in his arms the damp form of the dishevelled naiad. On her recovery — which was effected by Mr. Bouncer giving way under his burden, and lowering it to the ground — she utterly refused to be again carried in the wagon; and, as walking was perhaps better for her under the circumstances, she and Mr. Poletiss were escorted in procession to the inn hard by, where dry changes of costume were provided for them by the landlord and his fair daughter.

As this little misadventure was believed by all, save the privileged few, to have been purely the result of accident, it was not permitted, so Mr. Bouncer said, to do as Miss Morkin had done by him — throw a damp upon the party; and as the couple who had taken a watery bath met with great sympathy, they had no reason to complain of the incident. Especially had the fair Miss Morkin cause to rejoice therein, for the mild Mr. Poletiss had to make her so many apologies for having been the innocent cause of her fall, and, as a reparation, felt bound to so particularly devote himself to her for the remainder of the evening, that Miss Morkin was in the highest state of feminine gratification, and observed to her sister, when they were preparing themselves for rest, 'I am quite sure, Letitia Jane, that the gipsy woman spoke the truth, and could read the stars and whatdyecallems as easy as *a b c*. She told me that I should be married to a man with light whiskers and a soft voice, and that he would come to me from over the water; and it's quite evident that she referred to Mr. Poletiss and his falling into the brook; and I'm sure if he'd have had a proper opportunity he'd have said something definite to-night.' So Miss Eleonora Morkin laid her head upon her pillow, and dreamt of bride-cake and wedding-favours. Perhaps another young lady under the same roof was dreaming the same thing!

A ball at Honeywood Hall terminated the pleasures of the day. The guests had brought with them a change of garments, and were therefore enabled to make their reappearance in evening costume. This quiet interval for dressing was the first moment that Verdant could secure for sitting down by himself to think over the events of the day. As yet the time was too early for him to reflect calmly on the step he had taken. His brain was in that kind of delicious stupor which we experience when, having been aroused from sleep, we again shut our eyes for a moment's doze. Past, present, and future were agreeably mingled in his fancies. One thought quickly followed upon another; there was no dwelling upon one special point, but a succession of crowding feelings chased rapidly through his mind, all pervaded by that sunny hue that shines out from the knowledge of love returned.

He could not rest until he had told his sister Mary, and made her a sharer in his happiness. He found her just without the door, strolling up and down the drive with Charles Larkyns, so he joined them; and, as they walked in the pleasant cool of the evening down a shady walk, he stammered out to them, with many blushes, that Patty Honeywood had promised to be his wife.

'Cousin Patty is the very girl for you!' said Charles Larkyns, 'the very best choice you could have made. She will trim you up and keep you tight, as old Tennyson hath it. For what says 'the fat-faced curate Edward Bull?'

''I take it, God made the woman for the
   man
And for the good and increase of the
   world.
A pretty face is well, and this is well,
To have a dame indoors, that trims us up
And keeps us tight.'

'Verdant, you are a lucky fellow to have won the love of such a good and honest-hearted girl, and if there is any room left to mould you into a better fellow than what you are, Miss Patty is the very one for the modeller.'

At the same time that he was thus being congratulated on his good fortune and happy prospects, Miss Patty was making a similar confession to her mother and sister, and receiving the like good wishes. And it is probable that Mrs. Honeywood made no delay in communicating this piece of family news to her liege lord and master; for when, half an hour afterwards, Mr. Verdant Green had screwed up his courage sufficiently to enable him to request a private interview with Mr. Honeywood in the library, the Squire most humanely relieved him from a large load of embarrassment, and checked the hems and hums and haws that our hero was letting off like squibs, to enliven his conversation, by saying, 'I think I guess the nature of your errand — to ask my consent to your engagement with my daughter Martha? Am I right?'

And so, by this grateful helping of a very lame dog over a very difficult stile, the diplomatic relations and circumlocutions that are usually observed at horrible interviews of this description were altogether avoided, and the business was speedily brought to a satisfactory termination.

When Mr. Verdant Green issued from the library, he felt himself at least ten years older and a much more important person than when he had entered it, so greatly is our bump of self-esteem increased by the knowledge that there is a being in existence who holds us dearer than aught else in the whole wide world. But not even a misogynist would have dared to assert that, in the present instance, love was but an excess of self-love; for if ever there was a true attachment that honestly sprang from the purest feelings of the heart, it was that which existed between Miss Patty Honeywood and Mr. Verdant Green.

What need to dwell further on the daily events of that happy time? What need to tell how the several engagements of the two Miss Honeywoods were made known, and how, with Miss Mary Green and Mr. Charles Larkyns, there were thus three *bona fide* 'engaged couples' in the house at the same time, to say nothing of what looked like an embryo engagement between Miss Fanny Green and Mr. Bouncer? But if this last-named attachment should come to anything, it would probably be owing to the severe aggravation which the little gentleman felt on continually finding himself *de trop* at some scene of tender sentiment.

If, for example, he entered the library, its tenants, perhaps, would be Verdant and Patty, who would be discovered, with agitated expressions, standing or sitting at intervals of three yards, thereby endeavouring to convey to the spectator the idea that those positions had been relatively maintained by them up to the moment of his entering the room, an idea which the spectator invariably rejected. When Mr. Bouncer had retired with figurative Eastern apologies from the library, he would perhaps enter the drawing-room, there to find that Frank Delaval and Miss Kitty Honeywood had sprung into remote positions (as certain bodies rebound upon contact), and were regarding him as an unwelcome intruder. Thence, with more apologies, he would betake himself to the breakfast-room, to see what was going on in that quarter, and there he would flush a third brace of betrotheds, a proceeding that was not much sport to either party. It could hardly be a matter of surprise, therefore, if Mr. Bouncer should be seized with the prevailing epidemic, and, from the circumstances of his position, should be driven more than he might otherwise have been into Miss Fanny Green's society. And though the little gentleman had no serious intentions in all this, yet it seemed highly probable that something might come of it, and that Mr. AlFrank Brindle (whose attentions at the Christmas charade-party at the Manor Green had been of so marked a character) would have to resign his pretensions to Miss Fanny Green's hand in favour of Mr. Henry Bouncer.

But it is needless to describe the daily lives of these betrothed couples — how they rode, and sketched, and walked, and talked, and drove, and fished, and shot, and visited, and pic-nic'd — how they went out to sea in

Frank Delaval's yacht, and were overtaken by rough weather, and became so unromantically ill that they prayed to be put on shore again — how, on a chosen day, when the sea was as calm as a duckpond, they sailed from Bamborough to the Longstone, and nevertheless took provisions with them for three days, because, if storms should arise, they might have found it impossible to put back from the island to the shore; but how, nevertheless, they were altogether fortunate, and had not to lengthen out their pic-nic to such an uncomfortable extent — and how they went over the Lighthouse, and talked about the brave and gentle Grace Darling; and how that handsome, grey-headed old man, her father, showed them the presents that had been sent to his daughter by Queen, and Lords, and Commons, in token of her deed of daring; and how he was garrulous about them and her, with the pardonable pride of a

'fond old man,
Fourscore and upward,'

who had been the father of such a daughter. It is needless to detail all this; let us rather pass to the evening of the day preceding that which should see the group of visitors on their way back to Warwickshire.

Mr. Verdant Green and Miss Patty Honeywood have been taking a farewell after-dinner stroll in the garden, and have now wandered into the deserted breakfast-room, under the pretence of finding a water-colour drawing of Honeywood Hall, that the young lady had made for our hero.

'Now, you must promise me,' she said to him, 'that you will take it to Oxford.'

'Certainly, if I go there again. But — '

'*But*, sir! but I thought you had promised to give up to me on that point. You naughty boy! if you already break your promises in this way, who knows but what you will forget your promise to remember me when you have gone away from here?'

Mr. Verdant Green here did what is usual in such cases. He kissed the young lady, and said, 'You silly little woman! as though I *could* forget you!' *et cetera, et cetera.*

'Ah! I don't know,' said Miss Patty.

Mr. Verdant Green repeated the kiss and the *et ceteras*.

'Very well, then, I'll believe you,' at length said Miss Patty. 'But I won't love you one bit unless you'll faithfully promise that you will go back to Oxford. Whatever would be the use of your giving up your studies?'

'A great deal of use; we could be married at once.'

'Oh no, we couldn't. Papa is quite firm on this point. You know that he thinks us much too young to be married.'

'But,' pleaded our hero, 'if we are old enough to fall in love, surely we must be old enough to be married.'

'Oxford logic again, I suppose,' laughed Miss Patty, 'but it won't persuade papa, nevertheless. I am not quite nineteen, you know, and papa has always said that I should never be married until I was one-and-twenty. By that time you will have done with college and taken your degree, and I should so like to know that you have passed all your examinations, and are a Bachelor of Arts.'

'But,' said Verdant, 'I don't think I shall be able to pass. Examinations are very nervous affairs, and suppose I should be plucked. You wouldn't like to marry a man who had disgraced himself.'

'Do you see that picture?' asked Miss Patty; and she directed Verdant's attention to a small but exquisite oil-painting by Maclise. It was in illustration of one of Moore's melodies, 'Come, rest in this bosom, my own stricken deer!' The lover had fallen upon one knee at his mistress's feet, and was locked in her embrace. With a look of fondest love she had pillowed his head upon her bosom, as if to assure him, 'Though the herd have all left thee, thy home it is here.'

'Do you see that picture?' asked Miss Patty. 'I would do as she did. If all others rejected you yet would I never. You would still find your home here,' and she nestled fondly to his side.

'But,' she said, after one of those delightful pauses which lovers know so well how to fill up, 'you must not conjure up such silly fancies. Charles has often told me how easily you passed your — Little-go, isn't it called? — and he says you will have no trouble in obtaining your degree.'

'But two years is such a tremendous time to wait,' urged our hero, who, like all lovers, was anxious to crown his happiness without much delay.

'If you are resolved to think it long,' said Miss Patty; 'but it will enable you to tell whether you really like me. You might, you know, marry in haste, and then have to repent at leisure.'

And the end of this conversation was, that the fair special-pleader gained her cause, and that Mr. Verdant Green consented to return to Oxford, and not to dream of marriage until two years had passed over his head.

The next night he slept at the Manor Green, Warwickshire.

10

Mr. Verdant Green is Made a Mason

Mr. Verdant Green and Mr. Bouncer were once more in Oxford, and on a certain morning had turned into the coffee-room of 'The Mitre' to 'do bitters,' as Mr. Bouncer phrased the act of drinking bitter beer, when said the little gentleman, as he dangled his legs from a table,

'Giglamps, old feller! you ain't a Mason.'

'A Mason! of course not.'

'And why do you say 'of course not'?'

'Why, what would be the use of it?'

'That's what parties always say, my tulip. Be a Mason, and then you'll soon see the use of it.'

'But I am independent of trade.'

'Trade? Oh, I twig. My gum, Giglamps! you'll be the death of me some fine day. I didn't mean a Mason with a hod of mortar; he'd be a hod-fellow, don't you see? — there's a fine old crusted joke for you — I meant a Mason with a petticut, a Freemason.'

'Oh, a Freemason. Well, I really don't seem to care much about being one. As far as I can see, there's a great deal of mystery and very little use in it.'

'Oh, that's because you know nothing about it. If you were a Mason you'd soon see the use of it. For one thing, when you go abroad you'd find it no end of a help to you. If you'll stand another tankard of beer I'll tell you an *apropos* tale.'

So when a fresh supply of the bitter beverage had been ordered and brought, little Mr. Bouncer, perched upon the table, and dangling his legs, discoursed as follows:—

'Last Long, Billy Blades went on to the continent, and in the course of his wanderings he came across some gentlemen who turned out to be bandits, although they wern't dressed in tall hats and ribbons, and scarves, and watches, and velvet sit-upons, like you see them in pictures and at theatres; but they were rough customers for all that, and they laid hands upon Master Billy, and politely asked him for his money or his life.

'Billy wasn't inclined to give them either, but he was all alone, with nothing but his knapsack and a stick, for it was a frequented road, and he had no idea that there were such things as banditti in existence. Well, as you're aware, Giglamps, Billy's a modern Hercules, with an unusual development of biceps, and he not only sent out left and right, and gave them a touch of Hammer Lane and the Putney Pet combined, but he also applied his shoemaker to another gentleman's tailor with considerable effect. However, this didn't get him kudos, or mend matters one bit; and, after being knocked about much more than was agreeable to his feelings, he was forced to yield to superior numbers. They gagged and blindfolded him, formed him into a procession, and marched him off; and when in about half-an-hour they again let him have the use of his eyes and tongue, he found himself in a rude hut, with his banditti friends around him. They had pistols, and poniards, and long knives, with which they made threatening demonstrations. They had cut open his knapsack and tumbled out its contents, but not a *sou* could they find; for Billy, I should have told you, had left the place where he was staying, for a few days' walking tour, and he had only taken what little money he required; of this he had one or two pieces left, which he gave them. But it wouldn't satisfy the beggars, and they signified to him — for you see, Giglamps, Billy didn't understand a quarter of their lingo — that he must fork out with his tin unless he wished to be forked into with their steel. Pleasant position, wasn't it?'

'Extremely.'

'Well, they searched him, and when they found that they really couldn't get anything more out of him, they made him understand that he must write to some one for a ransom, and that he wouldn't be released until the money came. Pleasant again, wasn't it?'

'Excessively. But what has all this to do with Freemasonry?'

'Giglamps, you're as bad as a girl who peeps at the end of a novel before she begins to read it. Drink your beer, and let me tell my tale in my own way. Well, now we come to volume the third, chapter the last. Master Billy found that there was nothing for it but to obey orders, so he sent off a note to his banker, stating his requirements. As soon as this business was transacted, the amiable bandits turned to pleasure, and produced a bottle of wine, of which they politely asked Billy to partake. He thought at first that it might be poison, and he wasn't very far wrong, for it was most villainous stuff. However, the other fellows took to it kindly, and got more amiable than ever over it; so much so that they offered Billy one of his own weeds, and they all got very jolly, and were as thick as thieves. Billy made himself so much at home — he's a beggar that can always adapt himself to circumstances — that at last the chief bandit proposed his health, and then they all shook hands with him. Well, now comes the moral of my story. When the captain of the bandits was drinking Billy's Health in this flipper-shaking way, it all at once occurred to Billy to give him the Masonic grip. I must not tell you what it was, but he gave it, and, lo and behold! the bandit returned it. Both Billy and the bandit opened their eyes pretty considerably at this. The bandit also opened his arms and embraced his captive; and the long and short of it was that he begged Billy's pardon for the trouble and delay they had caused him, returned him his money and knapsack, and all the weeds that were not smoked, set aside the ransom, and escorted him back to the high road, guaranteeing him a free and unmolested passage if he should come that way again. And all this because Billy was a Mason; so you see, Giglamps, what use it is to a feller. But,' said Mr. Bouncer, as he ended his tale, 'talking's monstrously dry work. So, I looks to-wards you, Giglamps! to which, if you wish to do the correct thing, you should reply 'I likewise bows!'' And, little Mr. Bouncer, winking affably to his friend, raised the silver tankard to his lips, and kept it there for the space of ten seconds.

'I suppose,' said Verdant, 'that the real moral of your story is, that I must become a

Freemason, because I might travel abroad and be attacked by a scamp who was also a Freemason. Now, I think I had better decline joining a society that numbers banditti among its members.'

'Oh, but that was an exceptional case. I dare say, if the truth was known, Billy's friend had once been a highly respectable party, and had paid his water-rate and income-tax like any other civilized being. But all Masons are not like Billy's friend, and the more you know of them the more you'll thank me for having advised you to join them. But it isn't altogether that. Every Oxford man who is really a man is a Mason, and that, Giglamps, is quite a sufficient reason why *you* should be one.'

So Verdant said, Very well, he had no objection; and little Mr. Bouncer promised to arrange the necessary preliminaries. What these were will be seen if we advance the progress of events a few days later.

Messrs. Bouncer, Blades, Foote, and Flexible Shanks — who were all Masons, and could affix to their names more letters than members of far more learned societies could do — had undertaken that Mr. Verdant Green's initiation into the mysteries of the craft should be altogether a private one. Verdant felt that this was exceedingly kind of them; for, if it must be confessed, he had adopted the popular idea that the admission of members was in some way or other connected with the free use of a red-hot poker, and though he was reluctant to breathe his fears on this point, yet he looked forward to the ceremony with no little dread. He was therefore immensely relieved when he found that, by the kindness of his friends, his initiation would not take place in the presence of the assembled members of the Lodge.

For a week Mr. Verdant Green was benevolently left to ponder and speculate on the ceremonial horrors that would attend his introduction to the mysteries of Freemasonry, and by the appointed day he had worked himself into such a state of nervous excitement that he was burning more with the fever of apprehension than that of curiosity. There was no help for him, however; he had promised to go through the ordeal, whatever it might be, and he had no desire to be laughed at for having abandoned his purpose through fear.

The Lodge of Cemented Bricks, of which Messrs. Bouncer and Co. had promised to make Mr. Verdant Green a member, occupied spacious rooms in a certain large house in a certain small street not a hundred miles from the High Street. The ascent to the Lodge-room, which was at the top of the house, was by a rather formidable flight of stairs, up which Mr. Verdant Green tremblingly climbed, attended by Mr. Bouncer as his *fidus Achates*. The little gentleman, in that figurative Oriental language to which he was so partial, considerately advised his friend to keep up his pecker and never say die; but his exhortation of 'Now, don't you be frightened, Giglamps, we shan't hurt you more than we can help,' only increased the anguish of our hero's sensations; and when at the last he found himself at the top of the stairs, and before a door which was guarded by Mr. Foote, who held a drawn sword, and was dressed in unusually full Masonic costume, and looked stern and unearthly in the dusky gloom, he turned back, and would have made his escape had he not been prevented by Mr. 'Footelights'' naked weapon. Mr. Bouncer had previously cautioned him that he must not in any way evince a recognition of his friends until the ceremonies of the initiation were completed, and that the infringement of this command would lead to his total expulsion from his friends' society. Mr. Bouncer had also told him that he must not be surprised at anything that he might see or hear; which, under the circumstances, was very seasonable as well as

136

sensible advice. Mr. Verdant Green, therefore, submitted to his fate, and to Mr. Footelights' drawn sword.

'The first step, Giglamps,' whispered Mr. Bouncer, 'is the blindfolding; the next is the challenge, which is in Coptic, the original language, you know, of the members of the first Lodge of Cemented Bricks. Swordbearer and Deputy Past Pantile Foote will do this for you. I must go and put my things on. Remember, you musn't recognize me when you come into the Lodge. Adoo, Samiwel! keep your pecker up.' Mr. Verdant Green wrung his friend's hand, pocketed his spectacles, and submitted to be blindfolded.

Mr. Footelights then took him by the hand, and knocked three times at the door. A voice, which Verdant recognized as that of Mr. Blades, inquired, 'Kilaricum luricum tweedlecum twee?'

To which Mr. Footelights replied, 'Astrakansa siphonia bostrukizon!' and laid the cold steel blade against Mr. Verdant Green's cheek in a way which made that gentleman shiver.

Mr. Blades' voice then said, 'Swordbearer and Deputy Past Pantile, pass in the neophyte who seeks to be a Cemented Brick'; and Mr. Verdant Green was thereupon guided into the room.

'Gropelos toldery lol! remove the handkerchief,' said the voice of Mr. Blades.

The glare from numerous wax-lights, reflected as it was from polished gold, silver, and marble, affected Mr. Verdant Green's bandaged eyes, and prevented him for a time from seeing anything distinctly, but on Mr. Foote motioning to him that he might resume his spectacles, he was soon enabled by their aid to survey the scene. Around him stood Mr. Bouncer, Mr. Blades, Mr. Flexible Shanks, and Mr. Foote. Each held a drawn and gleaming sword; each wore aprons, scarves, or mantles; each was decorated with mystic Masonic jewellery; each was silent and preternaturally serious. The room was large and was furnished with the greatest splendour, but its contents seemed strange and mysterious to our hero's eyes.

'Advance the neophyte! Oodiny dulipy sing!' said Mr. Blades, who walked to the other end of the room, stepped upon a dais, ascended his throne, and laid aside the sword for a sceptre. Mr. Foote and Mr. Flexible Shanks then took Mr. Verdant Green by either shoulder, and escorted him up the room with their drawn swords turned towards him, while Mr. Bouncer followed, and playfully prodded him in the rear.

In the front of Mr. Blades' throne there was a species of altar, of which the chief ornaments were a large sword, a skull and cross-bones, illuminated by a great wax light placed in a tall silver candlestick. Silver globes and pillars stood upon the dais on either side of the throne; and luxuriously-velveted chairs and rows of seats were ranged around. Before the altar-like erection a small funereal black and white carpet was spread upon the black and white lozenged floor; and on this carpet were arranged the following articles:— a money chest, a ballot box (very like Miss Bouncer's Camera), two pairs of swords, three little mallets, and a skull and cross-bones — the display of which emblems of mortality confirmed Mr. Verdant Green in his previously-formed opinion, that the Lodge-room was a veritable chamber of horrors, and he would willingly have preferred a visit to that 'lodge in some vast wilderness,' for which the poet sighed, and to have forgone all those promised benefits that were to be derived from Freemasonry.

But wishing could not save him. He had no sooner arrived in front of the skull and cross-bones than the procession halted, and Mr. Blades, rising from his throne, said, 'Let the Sword-bearer and Deputy Past Pantile, together with the Provincial Grand Mortar-board, do their duty! Ramohun roy azalea tong! Produce the poker! Past Grand Hodman, remain on guard!'

Mr. Foote and Mr. Flexible Shanks removed their hands and swords from Mr. Verdant Green, and walked solemnly down the room, leaving little Mr. Bouncer standing beside our hero, and holding the drawn sword above his head. Mr. Foote and Mr. Flexible Shanks returned, escorting between them the poker. It was cold! that was a relief. But how long was it to remain so?

'Past Grand Hodman!' said Mr. Blades, 'instruct the neophyte in the primary proceedings of the Cemented Bricks.'

At Mr. Bouncer's bidding, Mr. Verdant Green then sat down upon the lozenged floor, and held his knees with his hands. Mr. Flexible Shanks then brought to him the poker, and said, 'Tetrao urogallus orygometra crex!' The poker was then, by the assistance of Mr. Foote, placed under the knees and over the arms of Mr. Verdant Green, who thus sat like a trussed fowl, and equally helpless.

'Recite to the neophyte the oath of the Cemented Bricks!' said Mr. Blades.

'Ramphastidinae toco scolopendra tinnunculus cracticornis bos!' exclaimed Mr. Flexible Shanks.

'Do you swear to obey through fire and water, and bricks and mortar, the words of this oath?' asked Mr. Blades from his throne.

'You must say, I do!' whispered Mr.

Bouncer to Mr. Verdant Green, who accordingly muttered the response.

'Let the oath be witnessed and registered by Swordbearer and Deputy Past Pantile, Provincial Grand Mortar-board, and Past Grand Hodman!' said Mr. Blades; and the three gentlemen thus designated stood on either side of and behind Mr. Verdant Green, and, with theatrical gestures, clashed their swords over his head.

'Keemo kimo lingtum nipcat! let him rise,' said Mr. Blades; and the poker was thereupon withdrawn from its position, and Mr. Verdant Green, being untrussed, but somewhat stiff and cramped, was assisted upon his legs.

He hoped that his troubles were now at an end; but this pleasing delusion was speedily dispelled, by Mr. Blades saying — 'The next part of the ceremonial is the delivery of the red-hot poker. Let the poker be heated!'

Mr. Verdant Green went chill with dread as he watched the terrible instrument borne from the room by Mr. Foote and Mr. Flexible Shanks, while Mr. Bouncer resumed his guard over him with the drawn sword. All was quiet save a smothered sound from the other side of the door, which, under other circumstances, Verdant would have taken for suppressed laughter; but, the solemnity of the proceedings repelled the idea.

At length the poker was brought in, red-hot and smoking, whereupon Mr. Blades left his throne and walked to the other end of the room, and there took his seat upon a second throne, before which was a second altar, garnished — as Mr. Verdant Green soon perceived, to his horror and amazement — with a human head (or the representation of one) projecting from a black cloth that concealed the neck, and, doubtless, the marks of decapitation. Its ghastly features were clearly displayed by the aid of a wax light placed in a tall silver candlestick by its side.

Mr. Blades received the poker from Mr. Foote, and commanded the neophyte to advance. Mr. Verdant Green did so, and took up a trembling position to the left of the throne, while Mr. Foote and Mr. Flexible Shanks proceeded to the organ, which was to the right of the entrance door. Mr. Blades then delivered the poker to Mr. Verdant Green, who, at first, imagined that he was required to seize it by its red-hot end, but was greatly relieved in his mind when he found that he had merely to take it by the handle, and repeat (as well as he could) a form of gibberish that Mr. Blades dictated. Having done this he was desired to transfer the poker to the Past Grand Hodman — Mr. Bouncer.

He had just come to the joyful conclusion

that the much dreaded poker portion of the business was now at an end, when Mr. Blades ruthlessly cast a dark cloud over his gleam of happiness, by saying — 'The next part of the ceremony will be the branding with the red-hot poker. Let the organist call in the aid of music to drown the shrieks of the victim!' and, thereupon, Mr. Foote struck up (with the full swell of the organ) a heart-rending air that sounded like 'the cries of the wounded' from *the Battle of Prague*.

Now, it happened that little Mr. Bouncer — like his sister — was subject to uncontrollable fits of laughter at improper seasons. For the last half-hour he had suffered severely from the torture of suppressed mirth, and now, as he saw Mr. Verdant Green's climax of fright at the anticipated branding, human nature could not longer bear up against an explosion of merriment, and Mr. Bouncer burst into shouts of laughter, and, with convulsive sobs, flung himself upon the nearest seat. His example was contagious; Mr. Blades, Mr. Foote, and Mr. Flexible Shanks, one after another, joined in the roar, and relieved their pent-up feelings with a rush of uproarious laughter.

At the first Mr. Verdant Green looked surprised, and in doubt whether or no this was but a part of the usual proceedings attendant upon the initiation of a member into the Lodge of Cemented Bricks. Then the truth dawned upon him, and he blushed up to his spectacles.

'Sold again, Giglamps!' shouted little Mr. Bouncer. 'I didn't think we could carry out the joke so far, I wonder if this will be hoax the last for Mr. Verdant Green?'

'I hope so indeed!' replied our hero; 'for I have no wish to continue a Freshman all through my college life. But I'll give you full liberty to hoax me again — if you can.' And Mr. Verdant Green joined good-humouredly in the laughter raised at his own expense.

Not many days after this he was really made a Mason; although the Lodge was not that of the Cemented Bricks, or the forms of initiation those invented by his four friends.

11

Mr. Verdant Green Breakfasts with Mr. Bouncer, and Enters for a Grind

Little Mr. Bouncer had abandoned his intention of obtaining a *licet migrare* to 'the Tavern,' and had decided (the Dons being propitious) to remain at Brazenface, in the nearer neighbourhood of his friends. He had resumed his reading for his degree; and, at various odd times, and in various odd ways, he crammed himself for his forthcoming examination with the most confused and confusing scraps of knowledge. He was determined, he said, 'to stump the examiners.'

One day, when Mr. Verdant Green had come from morning chapel, and had been refreshed by the perusal of an unusually long epistle from his charming Northumbrian correspondent, he betook himself to his friend's rooms, and found the little gentleman — notwithstanding that he was expecting a breakfast party — still luxuriating in bed. His curly black wig reposed on its block on the dressing table, and the closely shaven skull that it daily decorated shone whiter than the pillow that it pressed; for although Mr. Bouncer considered that night-caps might be worn by 'long-tailed babbies,' and by 'old birds that were as bald as coots,' yet, he, being a young bird — though not a baby — declined to ensconce his head within any kind of white covering, after the fashion of the portraits of the poet Cowper. The smallness of Mr. Bouncer's dormitory caused his wash-hand-stand to be brought against his bed's head; and the little gentleman had availed himself of this conveniency, to place within the basin a blubbering, bubbling, gurgling hookah, from which a long stem curled in vine-like tendrils, until it found a resting place in Mr. Bouncer's mouth. The little gentleman lay comfortably propped on pillows, with his hands tucked under his head, and his knees crooked up to form a rest for a manuscript book of choice 'crams,' that had been gleaned by him from those various fields of knowledge from which the true labourer reaps so rich and ripe a store. Huz and Buz reposed on the counterpane, to complete this picture of Reading for a Pass.

'The top o' the morning to you, Giglamps!' he said, as he saluted his friend with a volley of smoke — a salute similar as to the smoke, but superior, in the absence of noise and slightness of expense, to that which would have greeted Mr. Verdant Green's approach had he been of the royal blood — 'here I am! sweating away, as usual, for that beastly examination.' (It was a popular fallacy with Mr. Bouncer, that he read very hard and very regularly.) 'I thought I'd cut chapel this morning, and coach up for my Divinity paper. Do you know who Hadassah was, old feller?'

'No! I never heard of her.'

'Ha! you may depend upon it, those are the sort of questions that pluck a man;' said Mr. Bouncer, who thought — as others like him have thought — that the getting up of a few abstruse proper names would be proof sufficient for a thorough knowledge of the whole subject. 'But I'm not going to let them gulph me a second time; though, they ought not to plough a man who's been at Harrow, ought they, old feller?'

'Don't make bad jokes.'

'So I shall work well at these crams, although, of course, I shall put on my examination coat, and trust a good deal to my cards, and watch papers, and shirt wristbands, and so on.'

'I should have thought,' said Verdant, 'that after those sort of crutches had broken down with you once, you would not fly to their support a second time.'

'Oh, I shall though! — I must, you know!' replied the infatuated Mr. Bouncer. 'The Mum cut up doosid this last time; you've no

147

idea how she turned on the main, and did the briny! and, I must make things sure this time. After all, I believe it was those Second Aorists that ploughed me.'

It is remarkable, that, not only in Mr. Bouncer's case, but in many others, also, of a like nature, gentlemen who have been plucked can always attribute their totally-unexpected failures to a Second Aorist, or a something equivalent to 'the salmon,' or 'the melted butter,' or 'that glass of sherry,' which are recognized as the causes for so many morning reflections. This curious circumstance suggests an interesting source of inquiry for the speculative.

'Well!' said Mr. Bouncer meditatively; 'I'm not so sorry, after all, that they cut up rough, and ploughed me. It's enabled me, you see, to come back here, and be jolly. I shouldn't have known what to do with myself away from Oxford. A man can't be always going to feeds and tea-fights; and that's all that I have to do when I'm down in the country with the Mum — she likes me, you know, to do the filial, and go about with her. And it's not a bad thing to have something to work at! it keeps what you call your intellectual faculties on the move. I don't wonder at thingumbob crying when he'd no more whatdyecallems to conquer! he was regularly used up, I dare say.'

Mr. Bouncer, upon this, rolled out some curls of smoke from the corner of his mouth, and then observed, 'I'm glad I started this hookah! 'the judicious Hooker,' ain't it, Giglamps? it is so jolly, at night, to smoke oneself to sleep, with the tail end of it in one's mouth, and to find it there in the morning, all ready for a fresh start. It makes me get on with my coaching like a house on fire.'

Here there was a rush of men into the adjacent room, who hailed Mr. Bouncer as a disgusting Sybarite, and, flinging their caps and gowns into a corner, forthwith fell upon the good fare which Mr. Robert Filcher had spread before them; at the same time carrying on a lively conversation with their host, the occupant of the bed-room. 'Well! I suppose I must turn out, and do tumbies!' said Mr. Bouncer. So he got up, and went into his tub; and presently, sat down comfortably to breakfast, in his shirt-sleeves.

When Mr. Bouncer had refreshed his inner man, and strengthened himself for his severe course of reading by the consumption of a singular mixture of coffee and kidneys, beef-steaks and beer; and when he had rested from his exertions, and had resumed his pipe — which was not 'the judicious Hooker,' but a short clay, smoked to a swarthy hue, and on that account, as well as from its presumed medicatory power, called 'the Black Doctor,' — just then, Mr. Smalls, and a detachment of invited guests, who had been to an early lecture, dropped in to breakfast. Huz and Buz, setting up a terrific bark, darted towards a minute specimen of the canine species, which, with the aid of a powerful microscope, might have been discovered at the feet of its proud proprietor, Mr. Smalls. It was the first dog of its kind imported into Oxford, and it was destined to set on foot a fashion that soon bade fair to drive out of the field those long-haired Skye-terriers, with two or three specimens of which species, he entered the room.

'Kill 'em, Lympy!' said Mr. Smalls to his pet, who, with an extreme display of pugnacity, was submitting to the curious and minute inspection of Huz and Buz. 'Lympy' was a black and tan terrier, with smooth hair, glossy coat, bead-like eyes, cropped ears, pointed tail, limbs of a cobwebby structure, and so diminutive in its proportions, that its owner was accustomed to carry it inside the breast of his waistcoat, as a precaution, probably, against its being blown away. And it was called 'Lympy,' as an abbreviation of 'Olympus,' which was the name derisively given to it for its smallness, on the *lucus a non lucendo* principle that miscalls the lengthy 'brief' of the barrister, the 'living' — not-sufficient-to-support-life — of the poor vicar, the uncertain 'certain age,' the unfair 'fare' and the son-ruled 'governor.'

'Lympy' was placed upon the table, in order that he might be duly admired; an exaltation at which Huz and Buz and the Skye-terriers chafed with jealousy. 'Be quiet, you beggars! he's prettier than you!' said Mr. Smalls; whereupon, a mild punster present propounded the canine query, 'Did it ever occur to a cur to be lauded to the Skyes?' at which there was a shout of indignation, and he was sconced by the unanimous vote of the company.

'Lympy ain't a bad style of dog,' said little Mr. Bouncer, as he puffed away at the Black Doctor. 'He'd be perfect, if he hadn't one fault.'

'And what's his fault, pray?' asked his anxious owner.

'There's rather too much of him!' observed Mr. Bouncer, gravely. 'Robert!' shouted the little gentleman to his scout; 'Robert! doose take the feller, he's always out of the way when he's wanted.' And, when the performance of a variety of octaves on the post-horn, combined with the free use of the speaking-trumpet, had brought Mr. Robert Filcher to his presence, Mr. Bouncer received him with objurgations, and ordered another tankard of beer from the buttery.

In the mean time, the conversation had taken a sporting turn. 'Do you meet Drake's to-morrow?' asked Mr. Blades of Mr. Four-in-hand Fosbrooke.

'No! the old Berkshire,' was the reply.

'Where's the meet?'

'At Buscot Park. I send my horse to Thompson's, at the Farringdon-Road station, and go to meet him by rail.'

'And, what about the Grind?' asked Mr. Smalls of the company generally.

'Oh yes!' said Mr. Bouncer, 'let us talk over the Grind. Giglamps, old feller, you must join.'

'Certainly, if you wish it,' said Mr. Verdant Green, who, however, had as little idea as the man in the moon what they were talking about. But, as he was no longer a Freshman, he was unwilling to betray his ignorance on any matter pertaining to college life; so, he looked much wiser than he felt, and saved himself from saying more on the subject, by sipping a hot spiced draught, from a silver cup that was pushed round to him.

'That's the very cup that Four-in-hand Fosbrooke won at the last Grind,' said Mr. Bouncer.

'Was it indeed!' safely answered Mr.

Verdant Green, who looked at the silver cup (on which was engraven a coat of arms with the words 'Brazenface Grind. — Fosbrooke,'), and wondered what 'a Grind' might be. A medical student would have told [him] that a 'Grind' meant the reading up for an examination [under] the tuition of one who was familiarly termed 'a Grinder' — a process which Mr. Verdant Green's friends would phrase as 'Coaching' under 'a Coach;' but the conversation that followed upon Mr. Smalls' introduction of the subject, made our hero aware, that, to a University man, a Grind did not possess any reading signification, but a riding one. In fact, it was a steeple-chase, slightly varying in its details according to the college that patronized the pastime. At Brazenface, 'the Grind' was usually over a known line of country, marked out with flags by the gentleman (familiarly known as Anniseed) who attended to this business, and full of leaps of various kinds, and various degrees of stiffness. By sweepstakes and subscriptions, a sum of from ten to fifteen pounds was raised for the purchase of a silver cup, wherewith to grace the winner's wines and breakfast parties; but, as the winner had occasionally been known to pay as much as fifteen pounds for the day's hire of the blood horse who was to land him first at the goal, and as he had, moreover, to discharge many other little expenses, including the by no means little one of a dinner to the losers, the conqueror for the cup usually obtained more glory than profit.

'I suppose you'll enter *Tearaway*, as before?' asked Mr. Smalls of Mr. Fosbrooke.

'Yes! for I want to get him in condition for the Aylesbury steeple-chase,' replied the owner of *Tearaway*, who was rather too fond of vaunting his blue silk and black cap before the eyes of the sporting public.

'You've not much to fear from this man,' said Mr. Bouncer, indicating (with the Black Doctor) the stalwart form of Mr. Blades. 'Billy's too big in the Westphalias. Giglamps, you're the boy to cook Fosbrooke's goose. Don't you remember what old father-in-law Honeywood told you, — that you might, would, should, and could, ride like a Shafto? and lives there a man with soul so dead, — as Shikspur or some other cove observes — who wouldn't like to show what stuff he was made of? I can put you up to a wrinkle,' said the little gentleman, sinking his voice to a whisper. 'Tollitt has got a mare who can lick *Tearaway* into fits. She is as easy as a chair, and jumps like a cat. All that you have to do is to sit back, clip the pig-skin, and send her at it; and, she'll take you over without touching a twig. He'd promised her to me, but I intend to cut the Grind altogether; it interferes too much, don't you see, with my coaching. So I can make Tollitt keep her for you. Think how well the cup would look on your side-board, when you've blossomed into a parient, and changed the adorable Patty into Mrs. Verdant. Think of that, Master Giglamps!'

Mr. Bouncer's argument was a persuasive one, and Mr. Verdant Green consented to be one of the twelve gentlemen, who cheerfully paid their sovereigns to be allowed to make their appearance as amateur jockeys at the forthcoming Grind. After much debate, 'the Wet Ensham course' was decided upon; and three o'clock in the afternoon of that day fortnight was fixed for the start. Mr. Smalls gained *kudos* by offering to give the luncheon at his rooms; and the host of the Red Lion, at Ensham, was ordered to prepare one of his very best dinners, for the winding up of the day's sport.

'I don't mind paying for it,' said Verdant to Mr. Bouncer, 'if I can but win the cup, and show it to Patty, when she comes to us at Christmas.'

'Keep your pecker up, old feller! and put your trust in old beans,' was Mr. Bouncer's reply.

12

Mr. Verdant Green Takes His Degree

During the fortnight that intervened between Mr. Bouncer's breakfast party and the Grind, Mr. Verdant Green got himself into training for his first appearance as a steeple-chase rider, by practising a variety of equestrian feats over leaping-bars and gorse stuck hurdles; in which he acquitted himself with tolerable success, and came off with fewer bruises than might have been expected. At this period of his career, too, he strengthened his bodily powers by practising himself in those varieties of the 'manly exercises' that found most favour in Oxford.

The adoption of some portion of these was partly attributable to his having been made a Mason; for, whenever he attended the meetings of his Lodge, he had to pass the two rooms where Mr. MacLaren conducted his fencing-school and gymnasium. The fencing-room — which was the larger of the two, and was of the same dimensions as the Lodge-room above it — was usually tenanted by the proprietor and his assistant (who, as Mr. Bouncer phrased it, 'put the pupils through their paces,') and re-echoed to the sounds of stampings, and the cries of 'On guard! quick! parry! lunge!' with the various other terms of Defence and Attack, uttered in French and English. At the upper end of the room, over the fire-place, was a stand of curious arms, flanked on either side by files of single-sticks. The centre of the room was left clear for the fencing; while the lower end was occupied by the parallel bars, a regiment of Indian clubs, and a mattress apparatus for the delectation of the sect of jumpers.

Here Mr. Verdant Green, properly equipped for the purpose, was accustomed to swing his clubs after the presumed Indian manner, to lift himself off his feet and hang suspended between the parallel bars, to leap the string on to the mattress, to be rapped and thumped with single-sticks and boxing-gloves by any one else than Mr. Blades (who had developed his muscles in a most formidable manner), and to go through his parades of *quarte* and *tierce* with the flannel-clothed assistant. Occasionally he had a fencing bout with the good-humoured Mr. MacLaren, who — professionally protected by his padded leathern *plastron* — politely and obligingly did his best to assure him, both by precept and example, of the truth of the wise old saw, 'mens sana in corpore sano.'

The lower room at MacLaren's presented a

very different appearance to the fencing-room. The wall to the right hand, as well as a part of the wall at the upper end, was hung around — not

'With pikes, and guns, and bows,'

like the fine old English gentleman's, — but nevertheless,

'With swords, and good old cutlasses,'

and foils, and fencing masks, and fencing gloves, and boxing gloves, and pads, and belts, and light white shoes. Opposite to the door, was the vaulting-horse, on whose wooden back the gymnasiast sprang at a bound, and over which the tyro (with the aid of the spring-board) usually pitched himself headlong. Then, commencing at the further end, was a series of poles and ropes — the turning pole, the hanging poles, the rings, and the *trapeze*, — on either or all of which the pupil could exercise himself; and, if he had the skill so to do, could jerk himself from one to the other, and finally hang himself upon the sloping ladder, before the momentum of his spring had passed away.

Mr. Bouncer, who could do most things with his hands and feet, was a very distinguished pupil of Mr. MacLaren's; for the little gentleman was as active as a monkey, and — to quote his own remarkably figurative expression — was 'a great deal livelier than *the Bug and Butterfly.*'

Mr. Bouncer, then, would go through the full series of gymnastic performances, and finally pull himself up the rounds of the ladder, with the greatest apparent ease, much to the envy of Mr. Verdant Green, who, bathed in perspiration, and nearly dislocating every bone in his body, would vainly struggle (in attitudes like to those of 'the perspiring frog' of Count Smorltork) to imitate his mercurial friend, and would finally drop exhausted on the padded floor.

And, Mr. Verdant Green did not confine himself to these indoor amusements; but studied the Oxford Book of Sports in various out-of-door ways. Besides his Grinds, and cricketing, and boating, and hunting, he would paddle down to Wyatt's, for a little pistol practice, or to indulge in the exciting amusement of rifle-shooting at empty bottles, or to practise, on the leaping and swinging poles, the lessons he was learning at MacLaren's, or to play at skittles with Mr. Bouncer (who was very expert in knocking down three out of the four), or to kick football until he became (to use Mr. Bouncer's expression) 'as stiff as a biscuit.'

Or, he would attend the shooting parties given by William Brown, Esquire, of University House; where blue-rocks and brown rabbits were turned out of traps for the sport of the assembled bipeds and quadrupeds. The luckless pigeons and rabbits had but a poor chance for their lives; for, if the gentleman who paid for the privilege of the shot missed his rabbit (which was within the bounds of probability) the other guns were at once discharged, and the dogs of Town and Gown let slip. And, if any rabbit was nimble and fortunate enough to run this gauntlet with the loss of only a tail or ear, and, Galatea-like,

'fugit ad salices,'

and rushed into the willow-girt ditches, it speedily fell before the clubs of the 'cads,' who were there to watch, and profit by the sports of their more aristocratic neighbours.

Mr. Verdant Green would also study the news of the day, in the floating reading-room of the University Barge; and, from these comfortable quarters, indite a letter to Miss Patty, and look out upon the picturesque river with its moving life of eights and four-oars sweeping past with measured stroke. A great feature of the river picture, just about this time, was the crowd of newly introduced canoes;

their occupants, in every variety of bright-coloured shirts and caps, flashing up and down a double paddle, the ends of which were painted in gay colours, or emblazoned with the owner's crest. But Mr. Verdant Green, with a due regard for his own preservation from drowning, was content with looking at these cranky canoes, as they flitted, like gaudy dragon-flies, over the surface of the water.

Fain would the writer of these pages linger over these memoirs of Mr. Verdant Green. Fain would he tell how his hero did many things that might be thought worthy of mention, besides those which have been already chronicled; but, this narrative has already reached its assigned limits, and, even a historian must submit to be kept within reasonable bounds.

The Dramatist has the privilege of escaping many difficulties, and passing swiftly over confusing details, by the simple intimation, that 'An interval of twenty years is supposed to take place between the Acts.' Suffice it, therefore, for Mr. Verdant Green's historian, to avail himself of this dramatic art, and, in a very few sentences, to pass over the varied events of two years, in order that he may arrive at a most important passage in his hero's career.

The Grind came off without Mr. Verdant Green being enabled to communicate to Miss

Patty Honeywood, that he was the winner of a silver cup. Indeed, he did not arrive at the winning post until half an hour after it had been first reached by Mr. Four-in-hand Fosbrooke on his horse *Tearaway*; for, after narrowly escaping a blow from the hatchet of an irate agriculturist who professed great displeasure at any one presuming to come a galloperin' and a tromplin' over his fences, Mr. Verdant Green finally 'came to grief,' by being flung into a disagreeably moist ditch. And though, for that evening, he forgot his troubles, in the jovial dinner that took place at *the Red Lion*, yet, the next morning, they were immensely aggravated, when the Tutor told them that he had heard of the steeple-chase, and should expel every gentleman who had taken part in it. The Tutor, however, relented, and did not carry out his threat; though Mr. Verdant Green suffered almost as much as if he had really kept it.

The infatuated Mr. Bouncer madly persisted (despite the entreaties and remonstrances of his friends) in going into the Schools clad in his examination coat, and padded over with a host of crams. His fate was a warning that similar offenders should lay to heart, and profit by; for the little gentleman was again plucked. Although he was grieved at this on 'the Mum's' account, his mercurial temperament enabled him to thoroughly enjoy the Christmas vacation at the Manor Green, where were again gathered together the same party who had met there the previous Christmas. The cheerful society of Miss Fanny Green did much, probably, towards restoring Mr. Bouncer to his usual happy frame of mind; and, after Christmas, he gladly returned to his beloved Oxford, leaving Brazenface, and migrating ('through circumstances over which he had no control,' as he said) to 'the Tavern.' But when the time for his examination drew on, the little gentleman was seized with such trepidation, and 'funked' so greatly, that he came to the resolution not to trouble the Examiners again, and to dispense with the honours of a Degree. And so, at length, greatly to Mr. Verdant Green's sorrow, and 'regretted by all that knew him,' Mr. Bouncer sounded his final octaves and went the complete unicorn for the last time in a College quad, and gave his last Wine (wherein he produced some 'very old port, my teacakes! — I've had it since last term!') and then, as an undergraduate, bade his last farewell to Oxford, with the parting declaration, that, though he had not taken his Degree, yet that he had got through with great *credit*, for that he had left behind him a heap of unpaid bills.

By this time, or shortly after, many of Mr. Verdant Green's earliest friends had taken their Degrees, and had left College; and their places were occupied by a new set of men, among whom our hero found many pleasant companions, whose names and titles need not be recorded here.

When June had come, there was a 'grand Commemoration,' and this was quite a sufficient reason that the Miss Honeywoods should take their first peep at Oxford, at so favourable an opportunity. Accordingly there they came, together with the Squire, and were met by a portion of Mr. Verdant Green's family, and by Mr. Bouncer; and there were they duly taken to all the lions, and initiated into some of the mysteries of College life. Miss Patty was enchanted with everything that she saw — even carrying her admiration to Verdant's undergraduate's gown — and was proudly escorted from College to College by her enamoured swain.

'Pleasant it was, when woods were green,
And winds were soft and low,'

when in a House-boat, and in four-oars, they made an expedition ('a wine and water party,' as Mr. Bouncer called it) to Nuneham, and, after safely passing through the perils of the pound-locks of Iffley and Sandford, arrived at the pretty thatched cottage, and pic-nic'd in the round-house, and strolled through the nut plantations up to Carfax hill, to see the glorious view of Oxford, and looked at the Conduit, and Bab's-tree, and paced over the little rustic bridge to the island, where Verdant and Patty talked as lovers love to talk.

Then did Mr. Verdant Green accompany his lady-love to Northumberland; from whence, after spending a pleasant month that, all too quickly, came to an end, he departed (*via* Warwickshire) for a continental tour, which he took in the company of Mr. and Mrs. Charles Larkyns (*nee* Mary Green), who were there for the honeymoon.

Then he returned to Oxford; and when the month of May had again come round, he went in for his Degree examination. He passed with flying colours, and was duly presented with that much-prized shabby piece of paper, on which was printed and written the following brief form:—

Green Verdant e Coll. AEn. Fac. *Die 28° Mensis Maii Anni 185-*
Examinatus, prout Statuta requirunt, satis-fecit nobis Examinatoribus.

```
             {J. Smith      }
Ita testamur {Gul. Brown}} Examinatores in
             {Jac. L. Jones } Literis Humanio-
             {R. Robinson} ribus
```

Owing to Mr. Verdant Green having entered upon residence at the time of his matriculation, he was obliged, for the present, to defer the putting on of his gown, and, consequently, of arriving at the *full* dignity of a Bachelor of Arts. Nevertheless, he had taken his Degree *de facto*, if not *de jure*; and he, therefore — for reasons which will appear — gave the usual Degree dinner, on the day of his taking his Testamur.

He also cleared his rooms, giving some of his things away, sending others to Richards's sale-rooms, and resigning his china and glass to the inexorable Mr. Robert Filcher, who would forthwith dispose of these gifts (much over their cost price) to the next Freshman who came under his care.

Moreover, as the adorning of College chimney-pieces with the photographic portraits of all the owner's College friends, had just then come into fashion, Mr. Verdant Green's beaming countenance and spectacles were daguerreotyped in every variety of Ethiopian distortion; and, being enclosed in miniature frames, were distributed as souvenirs among his admiring friends.

Then, Mr. Verdant Green went down to Warwickshire; and, within three months, travelled up to Northumberland on a special mission.

CHAPTER THE LAST

Mr. Verdant Green is Married and Done For

Lasthope's ruined Church, since it had become a ruin — which was many a long year ago — had never held within its mouldering walls so numerous a congregation as was assembled therein on one particular September morning, somewhere about the middle of the present century. It must be confessed that this unusual assemblage had not been drawn together to see and hear the officiating Clergyman (who had never, at any time, been a special attraction), although that ecclesiastical Ruin was present, and looked almost picturesque in the unwonted glories of a clean surplice and white kid gloves. But, this decorative appearance of the Ruin, coupled with the fact that it was made on a week-day, was a sufficient proof that no ordinary circumstance had brought about this goodly assemblage.

At length, after much expectant waiting, those on the outside of the Church discerned the figure of small Jock Muir mounted on his highly trained donkey, and galloping along at a tearing pace from the direction of Honey-wood Hall. It soon became evident that he was the advance guard of two carriages that were being rapidly whirled along the rough road that led by the rocky banks of the Swirl. Before small Jock drew rein, he had struggled to relieve his own excitement, and that of the crowd, by pointing to the carriages and shouting, 'Yon's the greums, wi' the t'other priest!' the correctness of which assertion was speedily manifested by the arrival of the 'grooms' in question, who were none other than Mr. Verdant Green and Mr. Frank Delaval, accompanied by the Rev. Mr. Larkyns (who was to 'assist' at the ceremony) and their 'best men,' who were Mr. Bouncer and a cousin of Frank Delaval's. Which quintet of gentlemen at once went into the Church, and commenced a whispered conversation with the ecclesiastical Ruin. These circumstances, taken in conjunction with the gorgeous attire of the gentlemen, their white gloves, their waistcoats 'equal to any emergency' (as Mr. Bouncer had observed), and the bows of white satin ribbon that gave a festive appearance to themselves, their carriage-horses, and postilions — sufficiently proclaimed the fact that a wedding — and that, too, a double one — was at hand.

The assembled crowd had now sufficient to engage their attention, by the approach of a very special train of carriages, that was brought to a grand termination by two travelling-carriages, respectively drawn by four greys, which were decorated with flowers and white ribbons, and were bestridden by gay postilions in gold-tasseled caps and scarlet jackets. No wonder that so unusual a procession should have attracted such an assemblage; no wonder that Old Andrew Graham (who was there with his well-favoured daughters) should pronounce it 'a brae sight for weak een.'

As the clatter of the carriages announced their near approach to Lasthope Church, Mr. Verdant Green — who had been in the highest state of excitement, and had distractedly occupied himself in looking at his watch to see if it was twelve o'clock; in arranging his Oxford-blue tie; in futilely endeavouring to button his gloves; in getting ready, for the fiftieth time, the gratuity that should make the Ruin's heart to leap for joy; in longing for brandy and water; and in attending to the highly-out-of-place advice of Mr. Bouncer, relative to the sustaining of his 'pecker' — Mr. Verdant Green was thereupon seized with the fearful apprehension that he had lost the ring; and, after an agonizing and trembling search in all his pockets, was only relieved by finding it in his glove (where he had put it for safety) just as the double bridal procession entered the church.

Of the proceedings of the next hour or two, Mr. Verdant Green never had a clear perception. He had a dreamy idea of seeing a bevy of ladies and gentlemen pouring into the church, in a mingled stream of bright-coloured silks and satins, and dark-coloured broadcloths, and lace, and ribbons, and mantles, and opera cloaks, and bouquets; and, that this bright stream, followed by a rush of dark shepherd's-plaid waves, surged up the aisle, and, dividing confusedly, shot out from their centre a blue coat and brass buttons (in which, by the way, was Mr. Honeywood), on the arms of which were hanging two white-robed figures, partially shrouded with Honiton-lace veils, and crowned with orange blossoms.

Mr. Verdant Green has a dim remembrance of the party being marshalled to their places by a confused clerk, who assigned the wrong brides to the wrong bridegrooms, and appeared excessively anxious that his mistake should not be corrected. Mr. Verdant Green also had an idea that he himself was in that state of mind in which he would passively have allowed himself to be united to Miss Kitty Honeywood, or to Miss Letitia Jane Morkin (who was one of Miss Patty's bridesmaids), or to Mrs. Hannah More, or to the Hottentot Venus, or to any one in the female shape who might have thought proper to take his bride's place. Mr. Verdant Green also had a general recollection of making responses, and feeling much as he did when in for his *viva voce* examination at college; and of experiencing a difficulty when called upon to place the ring on one of the fingers of the white hand held forth to him, and of his probable selection of the thumb for the ring's resting place, had not the bride considerately poked out the proper finger, and assisted him to place the golden circlet in its assigned position. Mr. Verdant Green had also a misty idea that the service terminated with kisses, tears, and congratulations; and, that there was a great deal of writing and signing of names in two documentary-looking books; and that he had mingled feelings that it was all over, that he was made very happy, and that he wished he could forthwith project himself into the middle of the next week.

Mr. Verdant Green had also a dozy idea that he was guided into a carriage by a hand that lay lovingly upon his arm; and, that he shook a variety of less delicate hands that there were thrust out to him in hearty northern fashion; and, that the two cracked old bells of Lasthope Church made a lunatic attempt to ring a wedding peal, and only succeeded in producing music like to that which attends the hiving of bees; and, that he jumped into the carriage, amid a burst of cheering and God-blessings; and, that he heard the carriage-steps and door shut to with a clang; and that he felt a sensation of being whirled on by moving figures, and sliding scenery; and, that he found the carriage tenanted by one other person, and that person, his WIFE.

'My darling wife! My dearest wife! My own wife!' It was all that his heart could find to say. It was sufficient, for the present, to ring the tuneful changes on that novel word, and to clasp the little hand that trembled under its load of happiness, and to press that little magic circle, out of which the necromancy of Marriage should conjure such wonders and delights.

The wedding breakfast — which was attended, among others, by Mr. and Mrs. Poletiss (*nee* Morkins), and by Charles Larkyns and his wife, who was now

'The mother of the sweetest little maid
That ever crow'd for kisses,' —

the wedding breakfast, notwithstanding that it was such a substantial reality, appeared to Mr. Verdant Green's bewildered mind to resemble somewhat the pageant of a dream. There was the usual spasmodic gaiety of conversation that is inherent to bridal banquets,

173

and toasts were proclaimed and honoured, and speeches were made — indeed, he himself made one, of which he could not recall a word. Sufficient let it be for our present purpose, therefore, to briefly record the speech of Mr. Bouncer, who was deputed to return thanks for the duplicate bodies of bridesmaids.

Mr. Bouncer (who with some difficulty checked his propensity to indulge in Oriental figurativeness of expression) was understood to observe, that on interesting occasions like the present, it was the custom for the youngest groomsman to return thanks on behalf of the bridesmaids; and that he, not being the youngest, had considered himself safe from this onerous duty. For though the task was a pleasing one, yet it was one of fearful responsibility. It was usually regarded as a sufficiently difficult and hazardous experiment, when one single gentleman attempted to express the sentiments of one single lady; but when, as in the present case, there were ten single ladies, whose unknown opinions had to be conveyed through the medium of one single gentleman, then the experiment became one from which the boldest heart might well shrink. He confessed that he experienced these emotions of timidity on the present occasion. (*Cries of 'Oh!'*) He felt, that to adequately discharge the duties entrusted would require the might of an engine of ten-bridesmaid power. He would say more, but his feelings overcame him. (*Renewed cries of 'Oh!'*) Under these circumstances he thought that he had better take his leave of the subject, convinced that the reply to the toast would be most eloquently conveyed by the speaking eyes of the ten blooming bridesmaids. (*Mr. Bouncer resumes his seat amid great approbation.*)

Then the brides disappeared, and after a time made their re-appearance in travelling dresses. Then there were tears and 'doubtful joys,' and blessings, and farewells, and the departure of the two carriages-and-four (under a brisk fire of old shoes) to the nearest railway station, from whence the happy couples set out, the one for Paris, the other for the Cumberland Lakes; and it was amid those romantic lakes, with their mountains and waterfalls, that Mr. Verdant Green sipped the sweets of the honeymoon, and realized the stupendous fact that he was a married man.

★　★　★

The honeymoon had barely passed, and November had come, when Mr. Verdant Green was again to be seen in Oxford — a bachelor only in the University sense of the term, for his wife was with him, and they had rooms in the High Street. Mr. Bouncer was also there, and had prevailed upon Verdant to invite his sister Fanny to join them and be properly chaperoned by Mrs. Verdant. For, that wedding-day in Northumberland had put an effectual stop to the little gentleman's determination to refrain from the wedded state, and he could now say with Benedick, 'When I said I would die a bachelor, I did not think I should live till I were married.' But Miss Fanny Green had looked so particularly charming in her bridesmaid's dress, that little Mr. Bouncer was inspired with the notable idea, that he should like to see her playing first fiddle, and attired in the still more interesting costume of a bride. On communicating this inspiration (couched, it must be confessed, in rather extraordinary language) to Miss Fanny, he found that the young lady was far from averse to assisting him to carry out his idea; and in further conversation with her, it was settled that she should follow the example of her sister Helen (who was 'engaged' to the Rev. Josiah Meek, now the rector of a Worcestershire parish), and consider herself as 'engaged' to Mr. Bouncer. Which facetious idea of the little gentleman's was rendered the more amusing from its being accepted and agreed to by the young lady's parents and 'the Mum.' So here was Mr. Bouncer again in Oxford, an 'engaged' man, in company with the object of his affections, both being prepared as soon as possible to follow the example of Mr. and Mrs. Verdant Green.

Before Verdant could 'put on his gown,' certain preliminaries had to be observed. First, he had to call, as a matter of courtesy, on the head of his College, to whom he had to show his Testamur, and whose formal permission he requested that he might put on his gown.

'Oh yes!' replied Dr. Portman, in his mono-syllabic tones, as though he were reading aloud from a child's primer; 'oh yes, cer-tain-ly! I was de-light-ed to know that you had pass-ed and that you have been such a cred-it to your col-lege. You will o-blige me, if you please, by pre-sent-ing your-self to the Dean of Arts.' And then Dr. Portman shook hands with Verdant, wished him good morning, and re-sumed his favourite study of the Greek particles.

Then, at an appointed hour in the evening, Verdant, in company with other men of his college, went to the Dean of Arts, who heard them read through the Thirty-nine Articles, and dismissed them with this parting intimation — 'Now, gentlemen! I shall expect to see you at the Divinity School in the morning at ten o'clock. You must come with your bands and gown, and fees; and be sure, gentlemen, that you do not forget the fees!'

So in the morning Verdant takes Patty to the Schools, and commits her to the charge of Mr. Bouncer, who conducts her and Miss Fanny to one of the raised seats in the Convocation House, from whence they will have a good view of the conferring of Degrees. Mr. Verdant Green finds the precincts of the Schools tenanted by droves of college Butlers, Porters, and Scouts, hanging about for the usual fees and old gowns, and carrying blue bags, in which are the new gowns. Then — having seen that Mr. Robert Filcher is in attendance with his own particular gown — he struggles through the Pig-market, thronged with bustling Bedels and University Marshals, and other officials. Then, as opportunity offers, he presents himself to the senior Squire Bedel in Arts, George Valentine Cox, Esq., who sits behind a table, and, in his polite and scholarly manner, puts the usual questions to him, and permits him, on the due payment of all the fees, to write his name in a large book, and to place 'Fil. Gen.' after his autograph. Then he has to wait some time until the superior Degrees are conferred, and the Doctors and Masters have taken their seats, and the Proctors have made their apparently insane promenade.

Then the Deans come into the ante-chamber to see if the men of their respective Colleges are duly present, properly dressed, and have faithfully paid the fees. Then, when the Deans, having satisfactorily ascertained these facts, have gone back again into the Convocation House, the Yeoman Bedel rushes forth with his silver 'poker,' and summons all the Bachelors, in a very precipitate and far from impressive manner, with 'Now, then, gentlemen! please all of you to come in! you're wanted!' Then the Bachelors enter the Convocation House in a troop, and stand in the area, in front of the Vice-Chancellor and the two Proctors. Then are these young men duly quizzed by the strangers present, especially by the young ladies, who, besides noticing their own friends, amuse themselves by picking out such as they suppose to have been reading men, fast men, or slow men — taking the face as the index of the mind. We may be sure that there is a young married lady present who does not indulge in futile speculations of this sort, but fixes her whole attention on the figure of Mr. Verdant Green.

Then the Bedel comes with a pile of Testaments, and gives one to each man; Dr. Bliss, the Registrar of the University, administers to them the oath, and they kiss the book. Then the Deans present them to the Vice-Chancellor in a short Latin form; and then the Vice-Chancellor, standing up uncovered, with the Proctors standing on either side, addresses them in these words: 'Domini, ego admitto vos ad lectionem cujuslibet libri Logices Aristotelis; et insuper earum Artium, quas et quatenus per Statuta audivisse tenemini; insuper autoritate mea et totius universitatis, do vobis potestatem intrandi scholas, legendi, disputandi, et reliqua omnia faciendi, quae ad gradum Baccalaurei in Artibus spectant.'

When the Vice-Chancellor has spoken these remarkable words which, after three years of university reading and expense, grant so much that has not been asked or wished for, the newly-made Bachelors rush out of the Convocation House in wild confusion, and stand on one side to allow the Vice-Chancellarian procession to pass. Then, on emerging from the Pig-market, they hear St. Mary's bells, which sound to them sweeter than ever.

Mrs. Verdant Green is especially delighted with her husband's voluminous bachelor's gown and white-furred hood (articles which Mr. Robert Filcher, when helping to put them on his master in the ante-chamber, had declared to be 'the most becomingest things as was ever wore on a gentleman's shoulders'), and forthwith carries him off to be

180

photographed while the gloss of his new glory is yet upon him. Of course, Mr. Verdant Green and all the new Bachelors are most profusely 'capped;' and, of course, all this servile homage — although appreciated at its full worth, and repaid by shillings and quarts of buttery beer — of course it is most grateful to the feelings, and is as delightfully intoxicating to the imagination as any incense of flattery can be.

What a pride does Mr. Verdant Green feel as he takes his bride through the streets of his beautiful Oxford! how complacently he conducts her to lunch at the confectioner's who had supplied *their* wedding-cake! how he escorts her (under the pretence of making purchases) to every shop at which he has dealt, that he may gratify his innocent vanity in showing off his charming bride! how boldly he catches at the merest college acquaintance, solely that he may have the proud pleasure of introducing 'My wife!'

But what said Mrs. Tester, the bed-maker? 'Law bless you, sir!' said that estimable lady, dabbing her curtseys where there were stops, like the beats of a conductor's *baton* — 'Law bless you, sir! I've bin a wife meself, sir. And I knows your feelings.'

And what said Mr. Robert Filcher? 'Mr. Verdant Green,' said he, 'I'm sorry as how you've done with Oxford, sir, and that we're agoing to lose you. And this I *will* say, sir! if ever there was a gentleman I were sorry to part with, it's you, sir. But I hopes, sir, that you've got a wife as'll be a good wife to you, sir; and make you ten times happier than you've been in Oxford, sir!'

And so say we.

We do hope that you have enjoyed reading this large print book.

Did you know that all of our titles are available for purchase?

We publish a wide range of high quality large print books including:
Romances, Mysteries, Classics
General Fiction
Non Fiction and Westerns

Special interest titles available in large print are:
The Little Oxford Dictionary
Music Book
Song Book
Hymn Book
Service Book

Also available from us courtesy of Oxford University Press:
Young Readers' Dictionary
(large print edition)
Young Readers' Thesaurus
(large print edition)

For further information or a free brochure, please contact us at:
Ulverscroft Large Print Books Ltd.,
The Green, Bradgate Road, Anstey,
Leicester, LE7 7FU, England.
Tel: (00 44) **0116 236 4325**
Fax: (00 44) **0116 234 0205**

THE ADVENTURES OF MR. VERDANT GREEN

Cuthbert Bede

Young Mr. Verdant Green has tallied up eighteen years of unobjectionable existence at home with his sisters, comfortably insulated from the horrors of public school and the tyranny of sporting activities. But when Mr. Larkyns, local rector and Verdant's tutor, persuades Mr. Green Senior that his student is sorely in need of a little worldly experience, the callow Verdant is dispatched to Oxford for matriculation. As the innocent lamb embarks upon the odyssey of university life with characteristic trusting confidence, he finds himself gambolling into a den of wolves . . .